THE

SURVIVORS

THE

SURVIVORS

Alex Schulman

Translated from the Swedish by
Rachel Willson-Broyles

BOND
STREET
BOOKS

DOUBLEDAY
CANADA

Originally published in Sweden as *Överlevarna* by Albert Bonniers Förlag, Stockholm, in 2020. Copyright © 2020 by Alex Schulman.

This is a work of fiction. Names, characters, places, and incidents either are the product of the author's imagination or are used fictitiously. Any resemblance to actual persons, living or dead, events, or locales is entirely coincidental.

Bond Street Books and colophon are registered trademarks of Penguin Random House Canada Limited

Library and Archives Canada Cataloguing in Publication

Title: The survivors / Alex Schulman.
Other titles: Överlevarna. English
Names: Schulman, Alex, 1976- author.
Description: Translation of: Överlevarna.
Identifiers: Canadiana (print) 20210188324 | Canadiana (ebook) 20210188375 | ISBN 9780385697347 (hardcover) | ISBN 9780385697354 (EPUB)
Classification: LCC PT9877.29.C58 O9413 2021 | DDC 839.73/8—dc23

Book design by Anna B. Knighton
Jacket photograph by Albert Rösch / EyeEm / Getty Images
Jacket design by Emily Mahon

Printed in the United States of America

Published in Canada by Bond Street Books,
a division of Penguin Random House Canada Limited

www.penguinrandomhouse.ca

10 9 8 7 6 5 4 3 2 1

BOND STREET BOOKS | Penguin Random House Canada

For Calle and Niklas

1

THE COTTAGE

11:59 P.M.

A police car slowly plows through the blue foliage, down the narrow tractor path that leads to the property. There is the cottage, lonely on the point of land, in the June night that will never be entirely dark. It's a simple red wooden house, its proportions odd, a little taller than it should be. The white trim is flaking, and the siding on the south-facing wall has faded in the sun. The roofing tiles have grown together, the roof like the skin of a prehistoric creature. The air is still and it's a little chilly now; fog is collecting near the bottoms of the windowpanes. A single bright yellow light glows from one of the upstairs windows.

Down the slope is the lake, still and gleaming, edged with birches right down to the shore. And the sauna where the boys sat with their father on summer nights, staggering into the water afterward on the sharp rocks, walking in a line, balancing with their arms extended as if they had been crucified. "The water's nice!" their father shouted once he had thrown himself in, and his cry sang out across the lake, and the silence that followed existed nowhere but here, a place so far from everything else, a silence that sometimes frightened Benjamin but sometimes made him feel that everything was listening.

Farther along the shore is a boathouse; its lumber is decaying and the whole structure has started to lean toward the water. And above that is the barn, beams drilled with millions of termite holes and traces of seventy-year-old animal dung on the cement floor. Between the barn and the house is the small lawn where the boys used to play soccer. The ground slopes there; whoever plays with his back to the lake has an uphill battle.

This is the stage, this is how it looks, a few small buildings on a patch of grass with the forest behind it and the water in front. An inaccessible place, as lonely now as it was in years past. If you were to stand at the far end of the point and gaze out, you wouldn't see a hint of human life anywhere. Every rare once in a while they could hear a car passing on the gravel road across the lake, the distant sound of an engine in low gear; on dry summer days they could see the cloud of dust that rose from the forest soon after. But they never saw anyone; they were alone in this place they never left and where no one ever visited. Once they saw a hunter. The boys were playing in the forest and suddenly, there he was. A green-clad man with white hair, twenty yards away, slipping silently through the fir trees. As he passed, he looked blankly at the boys and brought his index finger to his lips and then he kept walking in among the trees until he was gone. There was never any explanation—he was like a mysterious meteor that passed close by but crossed the sky without making contact. The boys never talked about it afterward, and Benjamin sometimes wondered if it really happened.

It's two hours past dusk. The police car comes tentatively down the tractor path. The driver's anxious gaze is fixed just ahead of the hood, trying to see what sorts of things he's running down as he descends the hill, and even when he leans across the wheel and looks up he can't see the treetops. The evergreens that tower over the house are incredible. They were enormous even when the boys were small, but now they stretch a hundred to even a hundred and fifty feet into the air. The children's father was always proud of the fertile ground here, as if it were his doing. He stuck radish sprouts in the earth in early June and after just a few weeks he dragged the children to the garden to show them the rows of red dots rising out of the soil. But the fertile ground around the cottage can't be trusted; here and there the earth is completely dead. The apple tree Dad gave to Mom on her birthday still stands where he planted it once upon a time, but it never grows and it gives no fruit. In certain spots the soil is free of rocks, black and heavy. In others, the bedrock is just beneath the grass. Dad, when he was putting up a fence for the chickens, when he dragged the poker through the earth: sometimes it followed gentle and dull through the rain-heavy grass, sometimes it sang out just below the ground and he gave a shout, his hands vibrating with the resistance of the rock.

THE POLICE OFFICER climbs out of the car. His practiced movements as he quickly turns down the volume, muffling the strange chattering of the device on his shoulder. He's a big man.

The dinged, matte-black tools hanging at his waist make him look grounded somehow—their weight pulls him down to the crust of the earth.

Blue lights across the tall trees.

There's something about those lights, the mountains going blue across the lake and the blue lights of the police car—like an oil painting.

The policeman strides toward the house and stops. He's suddenly unsure of himself and takes a moment to observe the scene. The three men are sitting side by side on the stone steps that lead up to the front door of the cottage. They're crying, holding each other. They're wearing suits and ties. Next to them, on the grass, is an urn. He makes eye contact with one of the men, who stands. The other two remain seated, still in each other's arms. They're wet and badly beaten up, and he understands why an ambulance has been summoned.

"My name is Benjamin. I'm the one who called."

The officer searches his pockets for a notepad. He doesn't yet know that this story can't be written up on a blank page or two, that he's stepping in at the end of a tale that's spanned decades, a tale of three brothers who were torn away from this place long ago and now have been forced to return, that everything here is interconnected, that nothing stands alone nor can be explained on its own. The weight of what's taking place right now is enormous, but, of course, most of it has already happened. What's playing out here on these stone steps, the tears of three brothers, their swollen faces and all the blood, is only the last ripple on the water, the one farthest out, the one with the most distance from the point of impact.

2

THE SWIM RACE

Each evening Benjamin stood at the water's edge with his net
and his bucket, just up the shore from the little embankment
where his mother and father sat. They followed the evening sun,
shifting table and chairs by a few feet whenever they landed in
the shade, moving slowly as the evening went on. Under the table
sat Molly, the dog, watching in surprise as her roof disappeared,
then following the outfit on its journey along the shore. Now
his parents were at the final stop, watching the sun sink slowly
behind the treetops across the lake. They always sat next to each
other, shoulder to shoulder, because both of them wanted to
gaze out at the water. White plastic chairs drilled down into the
tall grass, a small, tilted wooden table where the smudged beer

glasses glinted in the evening sun. A cutting board with the butt of a winter salami, mortadella, and radishes. A cooler bag in the grass between them to keep the vodka cold. Each time Dad took a shot he said a quick "Hey" and raised the glass toward nothing and drank. Dad cut the salami so the table shook, beer sloshing, and Mom was immediately annoyed—she made a face as she held her glass in the air until he was done. His father never noticed any of this, but Benjamin did. He made note of every shift of theirs; he always kept a distance that allowed them peace and quiet even as he could still follow their conversation, keep an eye on the atmosphere and their moods. He heard their friendly murmurs, utensils against porcelain, the sound of one of them lighting a cigarette, a stream of sounds that suggested that everything was fine between them.

Benjamin walked along the shore with his net. Gazing down at the dark water, now and again he happened to glance directly at the reflection of the sun, and his eyes hurt as if they had burst. He balanced on the large rocks, inspecting the bottom for tadpoles, those strange creatures, tiny and black, sluggish swimming commas. He scooped some up in the net and took them captive in his red bucket. This was a tradition. He collected tadpoles near his parents as a façade, and when the sun went down and his parents stood to head back to the house again, he returned the tadpoles to the water and wandered up with Mom and Dad. Then he started all over again the next night. One time he forgot the tadpoles in the bucket. When he discovered them the next afternoon, they were all dead, obliterated in the sun's heat. Terror-stricken that Dad would find out, he dumped the contents into the lake, and although he knew that Dad was up in the cottage resting, it was as if his eyes were burning holes into the back of Benjamin's neck.

"Mom!"

BENJAMIN LOOKED UP at the house and saw his little brother coming down the hill. You could spot his impatience from here. This was no place for the restless. Especially not this year—upon their arrival a week earlier, their parents had decided that they wouldn't watch TV all summer. The children were apprised of this in solemn tones, and Pierre especially didn't take it well when Dad pulled out the plug of the TV and ceremoniously placed the end on top of the appliance, like after a public execution where the body is left hanging as a warning, so that everyone was reminded of what happened to technology that was a threat to the family's decision to spend the summer out-of-doors.

Pierre had his comic books, which he slowly read out loud to himself, mumbling on his belly in the grass in the evenings. But eventually he would get bored and make his way down to his parents, and Benjamin knew that Mom and Dad's reactions could vary; sometimes you were allowed to crawl onto Mom's lap and she would scratch your back gently. Other times, their parents grew annoyed and the moment was lost.

"I don't have anything to do," Pierre said.

"Don't you want to catch tadpoles with Benjamin?" Mom asked.

"No," he replied. He stood behind Mom's chair and squinted at the setting sun.

"Well, what about Nils, can't the two of you do something?"

"Like what?"

Silence. There they sat, Mom and Dad, weary somehow, collapsed in their plastic chairs, heavy with alcohol. They gazed out at the lake. It was like they were trying to think of something to say, activities to suggest, but no words came out.

"Hey," Dad muttered, throwing back a shot, and then he grimaced and clapped his hands sharply three times. "Okay then," he called out. "I want to see all my boys down here in bathing suits in two minutes!"

Benjamin looked up, took a few steps away from the edge of the water. Dropped his net in the grass.

"Boys!" Dad called. "Assemble!"

Nils was listening to his Walkman in the hammock that was strung between the two birches up by the house. While Benjamin paid careful attention to the sounds of their family, Nils shut them out. Benjamin was always trying to get closer to his parents; Nils wanted to get away. He would be in a different room, not joining in. At bedtime, the brothers could sometimes hear their parents arguing through the thin plywood wall. Benjamin registered each word, assessed the conversation to see what damage it would bring. Sometimes they shouted inconceivable cruelties at each other, said such harsh things that it felt irreparable. Benjamin would lie awake for hours, replaying the argument in his mind. But Nils seemed genuinely undisturbed. "Madhouse," he mumbled as the argument gained strength; then he turned over and fell asleep. He didn't care, kept to himself during the day, not making much of a stir—except for sudden outbursts of rage that flared up and faded again. "Fuck!" they might hear from the hammock as Nils began to lurch and wave his hands hysterically to shoo away a wasp that had come too close.

"Crazy fucking lunatics!" he roared, smacking at the air a few times. Then calm settled once more.

"Nils!" Dad called. "Assembly on the shore!"

"He can't hear you," Mom said. "He's listening to music."

Dad shouted louder. No reaction from the hammock. Mom sighed, stood up, and hurried over to Nils, flapping her arms in front of his face. He took off his headphones. "Dad wants you," she said.

Assembly on the shore. It was a golden moment. Dad with that special look in his eye that the brothers loved, a sparkle that promised fun and games, and always that same serious note in his voice when he was about to present a new competition, grave solemnity with a smile hiding at the corner of his mouth. Ceremonious and formal, as if there was much at stake.

"The rules are simple," he said, towering in front of the three brothers where they stood, skinny legs sticking out of their bathing trunks. "On my signal, my boys will leap into the water, swim around the buoy out there, and return to land. And the first one back wins."

The boys lined up.

"Everyone understand?" he said. "This is it—the moment we find out which brother is the fastest!"

Benjamin slapped his skinny thighs as he'd seen athletes do before crucial competitions on TV.

"Hold on," Dad said, taking off his watch. "I'll time you."

Dad's big thumbs poked at the tiny buttons of the digital watch, and he mumbled "Dammit" to himself when he couldn't get it to work. He glanced up.

"On your marks."

A scuffle between Benjamin and Pierre for the best starting position.

"No, stop it," Dad said. "None of that."

"Then let's just forget it," said Mom. She was still at the table, refilling her glass.

The brothers were seven, nine, and thirteen, and when they played soccer or cards together these days, sometimes their fights were so bad that Benjamin felt like something between them was breaking. The stakes were even higher when Dad pitted the brothers against each other, when he made it so clear that he wanted to find out which of his sons was best at something.

"On your marks . . . get set . . . go!"

Benjamin dashed for the lake with his two brothers close on his heels. Into the water. He heard shouts behind him, Mom and Dad cheering from the shore.

"Bravo!"

"Come on!"

A few quick steps and the sharp rocks disappeared beneath him. The cove had a June chill, and a little farther out were the strange bands of even colder water that came and went as if the lake were a living being that wanted to test him with different kinds of cold. The white Styrofoam buoy lay still on the mirrored surface ahead of them. The brothers had set it out a few hours earlier when they were dropping nets with their father. But Benjamin didn't remember its being so far out. They swam in silence, to preserve their energy. Three heads in the black water, the shouts from the beach fading into the distance. After a while the sun vanished behind the trees on the opposite side.

The light grew dim; they were suddenly swimming in a different lake. Without warning, Benjamin found the water foreign. All at once he was aware of everything happening beneath him, the creatures in the depths that might not want them there. He thought of all the times he'd sat in the boat with his brothers as Dad plucked fish from the net and tossed them into the bottom. And the brothers leaned in to look at the razor-sharp little fangs of the pike, the spiny fins of the perch. One of the fish flopped and the brothers jumped and shrieked, and Dad, startled by the sudden cries, shouted back in alarm. Then calm returned and he muttered as he wound up the nets, "You can't be afraid of fish." Now Benjamin thought about these beings swimming right alongside him, or just below him, hidden by the murky water. The white buoy, suddenly pink in the sunset, was still far away.

After a few minutes of swimming the starting lineup had spread out—Nils was well ahead of Benjamin, who had left Pierre behind. But when darkness fell and the chill began to sting their thighs, the brothers closed ranks again. Soon they were swimming in tight formation. Maybe it wasn't conscious, and maybe they would never admit it to each other, but they would not leave anyone behind in the water.

Their heads were sinking closer toward the surface. The reach of their arms became shorter. At first the water had frothed with the brothers' strokes, but now the lake was quiet. When they reached the buoy, Benjamin turned around to look at the cottage. The house looked like a red Lego brick in the distance. Only now did he realize how far the return trip was.

The exhaustion hit him out of nowhere. He couldn't lift his arms for all the lactic acid. He was so surprised that he seemed all of a sudden to have forgotten how to move his legs. A bolt of cold radiated from the back of his neck into his head. He could hear his own breaths, how they were growing shorter and more labored, and an icy realization filled his chest: he wasn't going to make it back to shore. He could see Nils craning his neck to keep from getting water in his mouth.

"Nils," Benjamin said. Nils didn't react, just kept swimming with his eyes on the sky. Benjamin made his way up to his older brother, and they breathed hard in each other's faces. Their eyes met and Benjamin saw a fear he didn't recognize in his brother's gaze.

"Are you okay?" Benjamin asked.

"I don't know . . ." he gasped. "I don't know if I can do this."

Nils reached for the buoy and held on to it with both hands to float on it, but it couldn't bear his weight and sank into the darkness beneath him. He gazed toward the land.

"I can't," Nils mumbled. "It's too far."

Benjamin searched his memory for what he'd learned in swimming lessons, during the instructor's long lectures on water safety.

"We have to stay calm," he told Nils. "Take longer strokes. Longer breaths."

He glanced at Pierre.

"How are you doing?" he asked.

"I'm scared," Pierre said.

"Me too," Benjamin replied.

"I don't want to die!" Pierre cried. His moist eyes just above the surface.

"Come here," Benjamin said. "Come by me." The three

brothers moved closer in the water. "We'll help each other," Benjamin said.

They swam side by side in the direction of the house.

"Long strokes," said Benjamin. "We'll take long strokes together."

Pierre had stopped crying and was now swimming doggedly alongside them. After a while they found a common rhythm, were taking common strokes, they breathed out and breathed in, long breaths.

Benjamin looked at Pierre and laughed. "Your lips are blue."

"Yours too."

They flashed quick grins at each other. And returned to concentrating. Head above the surface. Long strokes.

Benjamin saw the cottage far off, and the little field with its uneven grass where he played soccer with Pierre every day. The root cellar and berry bushes to the left, where they went out in the afternoons to pick raspberries and black currants and came back with white scratches all over their tanned legs. And behind all of this rose the firs, dark against the dusk.

The brothers drew close to the shore.

When they were only fifteen yards away, Nils sped up, crawling wildly. Benjamin cursed his sluggish surprise and set off after his brother. Suddenly the lake was no longer quiet, as the brothers' fierce battle to reach the shore intensified. Pierre was soon hopelessly behind. Nils was one stroke ahead of Benjamin when they reached land, and they ran up the hill side by side. Benjamin yanked at Nils's arm to pass, and Nils tore himself loose with a fury that shocked Benjamin. They made it to the patio. They looked around.

Benjamin took a few steps toward the house and peered through one of the windows. And there he caught a glimpse of Dad's figure. His broad back bent over the dishes.

"They went inside," Benjamin said.

Nils stood with his hands on his knees, catching his breath.

Pierre came up the hill, panting. His confused gaze aimed at the empty table. They stood there at a loss, the brothers. Three anxious breaths panting in the silence.

| **3** |

Nils shoves the urn with full force at his brother. Pierre isn't ready for it and it lands on his chest. From the crack, Benjamin knows immediately that something has broken inside Pierre's body. A rib or his sternum. Benjamin has always been able to see three steps ahead of everyone else. He could predict conflicts between the members of his family long before they happened. From the first moment of irritation, so subtle that it was hardly even there, he knew how the argument would begin and how it would end. But this is different. From this moment on, as something breaks inside Pierre's chest, he knows nothing. Everything starting now is uncharted territory. Pierre lies in the shallow water and holds his chest. Nils hurries to him: "Are you okay?"

He bends down to help his brother up. He's frightened.

Pierre kicks Nils in the calves so that he collapses on the rocky shore. Then Pierre throws himself on top of his older brother; they roll around and around, hammering their fists into faces and chests and shoulders. And all along, they speak. Benjamin finds the scene surreal, almost fantastical, how they're talking to each other even as they try to kill each other.

Benjamin picks up the urn, which has fallen by the embankment. The lid has come off, and some of the ash has spilled onto the sand. The color of the skeletal remains is gray, leaning purple, and he reacts very briefly to it as he picks up the urn and puts its lid back on; that's not how he imagined Mom's ashes. He holds on to the urn with both hands, takes a few steps back, going stiff as he is faced with his brothers' fight. Frozen on the sidelines, as was so often the case in the past. He observes their awkward punches, their clumsiness. On any other day, Pierre would beat his brother black and blue. He's been fighting since he was a teen. Memories from their school days, as Benjamin crossed the schoolyard and saw kids gathering to watch a fight, and between the down jackets Benjamin could see his brother bending over someone and he moved by quickly, never wanted to see his brother landing punch after punch even though his opponent was no longer moving, looked lifeless. Pierre can fight, but here at the water's edge the odds are evened out, because he's cracked a rib and can hardly stand upright. Most of the blows between the brothers meet only air, or don't quite land, or are parried with hands and arms. But a few of their attacks are devastating. Pierre gets Nils in the eye and right away Benjamin can see the blood trickling down his cheek and onto his neck. Nils elbows Pierre and it sounds like he breaks his nose.

Nils tears at Pierre's hair, and when he finally lets go, tufts of it dangle between his fingers. After a while, they grow tired. For an instant it seems as though neither of them has the strength to continue. They sit at the water's edge, a few yards between them, looking at each other. And then they start all over again. It's slow and drawn out; they want to kill each other but don't seem to be in any hurry.

And they keep talking.

Nils aims a kick at his brother but misses and loses his balance. Pierre backs away and picks up a rock from the beach, lobbing it at Nils. The rock whizzes by, but Pierre takes another and throws it and this time it hits Nils on the chin. More blood. Benjamin tentatively backs up and over the embankment, holding the urn so tightly that his fingers go white. He turns around and trudges up to the house. He goes inside, into the kitchen, and finds his phone. He calls the emergency number.

"My brothers are fighting," he says. "I'm afraid they're going to beat each other to death."

"Can you intervene?" asks the woman on the phone.

"No."

"Why not? Are you injured?"

"No, no . . ."

"Why can't you intervene?"

Benjamin presses the phone firmly to his ear. Why can't he intervene? He gazes out the window. He can see all of the little settings of his childhood. This landscape is where it all began, and this is where it ended. He can't intervene because he got stuck here once upon a time and hasn't been able to move since. He's still nine years old, and the men fighting down there are adults, the brothers who kept living.

He sees the shape of the two of them, trying to kill each other. It's no worthy finale, but perhaps it's also no surprise. How else had they expected this to end? What did they think would happen when they returned at last to the place they had spent their lives trying to flee? Now his brothers are fighting in knee-deep water. Benjamin watches as Pierre heaves Nils down under the surface. He stays there, doesn't get up, and Pierre makes no attempt to help him.

A thought passes through Benjamin: They're going to die down there.

And he drops the phone and now he's running. He dashes out and down the stone steps—the path to the lake is in his muscle memory; he can still dodge every obstacle, so even at high speed, he avoids every protruding root, jumps every sharp rock. He is running through his childhood. He passes the spot where his parents always sat in the last of the evening sun, before it set behind the lake. He makes his way past the wall of forest that rises to the east, passes the boathouse. He runs. When did he last do that? He doesn't recall. He has lived his adult life at a constant standstill, as if within parentheses, and now that he feels his heart pounding in his chest he is filled with a strange euphoria to find that he can run, that he has the energy, or, maybe, above all: that he wants to. He takes strength in the fact that something is finally driving him to act. And he jumps over the little ledge where he used to catch tadpoles as a child and throws himself into the water. He grabs his brothers and prepares to pull them apart, but he soon realizes that there's no need. They've stopped fighting. And they're standing close together in water up to their waists, a few yards out into the lake. They're looking at each other. Their dark hair is alike, they have identical eyes, the same chestnut brown. They don't speak. The lake grows quiet. Just the sound of three brothers crying.

On the stone steps they inspect each other's wounds. They don't apologize, because they don't know how, because no one has ever taught them. They cautiously feel each other's bodies, dab at cuts, they press their foreheads together. The three brothers hold each other.

Through the dull, humid summer silence, Benjamin suddenly hears a car engine in the forest above them. He glances over at the slope. A police car slowly plows through the blue foliage, down the narrow tractor path that leads to the property. There is the cottage, lonely on the point of land, in the June night that will never be entirely dark.

| **4** |

THE PILLAR OF SMOKE

Mom and Dad stood up after lunch on the patio. Dad gathered the plates and stacked the glasses. Mom brought the white wine into the kitchen and gingerly put the bottle in the fridge. Signs of life in the bathroom after that—the water pump howled a few times. Dad spat forcefully into the sink. Then they trooped upstairs, their steps heavy. Benjamin heard the bedroom door close, and it was quiet.

They called it their "siesta." Nothing strange about it, they'd informed the children—people in Spain did it all the time. An hour's nap after lunch, in order to face the evening fresh and alert. For Benjamin it was a long hour of nothing, followed by the peculiar half hour when Mom and Dad staggered back out to the patio, sitting silent and combustible in their plastic chairs. As a rule, Benjamin kept his distance then, letting them wake up in peace, but soon he approached his parents, and his brothers did too, from different parts of the yard, because once in a while, after the siesta, Mom would read aloud to the children. On a blanket on the lawn if the weather was nice, or on the kitchen bench before the fire if it was raining, the children sat in silence and listened as Mom read from old classics, the books she thought children should know. And it was just Mom's voice, there was nothing else, and she ran her free hand through a child's hair, and the longer this time lasted the closer the boys came to their mother, until at last it was like they were joined together, you couldn't tell where one child ended and the next began. When she reached the end of a chapter, she would close the book with a snap right in front of one of their noses, and they all screeched in delight.

Benjamin sat down on the stone steps. He had a long wait ahead of him. He gazed down at his banged-up summer legs, saw the mosquito bites on his shins, smelled the scent of his sunburned skin and the antiseptic Dad had dabbed onto his feet to treat his nettle stings. His heart beat faster even though he wasn't moving. It wasn't boredom he felt; it was something different, harder to explain. He was sad without quite knowing why. He gazed down the placid slope at the lake, the sunscorched, bleached meadow. And he felt everything around him falter. It was like a bell jar had been lowered over the point. His eyes followed a wasp as it anxiously circled a bowl of cream sauce that had been left on the table. The wasp was heavy and irrational and it was having problems, it looked like its wings were beating more and more slowly, with more and more effort, and then it got too close to the sauce and was caught. Benjamin followed its struggle to free itself, but little by little its movements slowed until at last they stopped. He listened to the birdsong, suddenly strange; it was as if the birds were singing more slowly, at half speed. Then they fell silent. Benjamin felt terror flow through him. Had time stopped? He clapped five times as he usually did to return to himself.

"Hello!" he called into the air. He stood up, clapped again, five times, so hard that his palms stung.

"What are you doing?"

Pierre was standing down by the lake and looking up at him. "Nothing," Benjamin replied.

"Want to go fishing?"

"Okay."

Benjamin went to the hall for his boots. Then he walked around the corner of the cottage to get the fishing rod that was leaning against the wall.

"I know where there are worms," said Pierre.

They went behind the barn, where the soil was moist. They turned over two shovelfuls and suddenly the ground was glistening with worms. The brothers pulled them from the soil and collected them in a jar, where they lay placidly, unconcerned about their captivity. Pierre shook the jar, turning it over to rouse them, but they seemed to take everything as it came— even death, because when Benjamin threaded them onto the hook down by the lake they didn't protest but let themselves be drilled through by the metal.

THEY TOOK TURNS holding the rod. The bobber was red and white and stood out clearly against the black water, except when it vanished into the spots of sun on the surface. Along the shore came the Larsson Sisters, the farm's three hens, in a group but each minding her own business, randomly pecking at the ground here and there, clucking softly. Benjamin had always felt uncomfortable when they came near him, because there was no logic to their behavior. He felt edgy, as if anything could happen—like when a wino suddenly spoke to you on the square. Plus, Dad had said one of them was blind, and might lose it if she felt threatened, and Benjamin would stare into the hens' empty eyes but could never tell which of them couldn't see. Weren't all of them blind, in fact? It looked like it as they crept nervously across the ground. Dad was the one who had bought the hens, a few summers ago, in order to finally fulfill his lifelong dream of eating freshly laid eggs for breakfast. Dad fed them, tossing the dry feed after them in the afternoon and calling, "Pot-pot-pot," and in the evenings he herded them into the barn, the sound of his ladle striking the bottom of a pan echoing across the whole property. Each morning Pierre had the task of fetching eggs from the Larsson Sisters' coop, and he'd come running back up the grassy path to the house with the treasure in his hands and Dad would hurry into the kitchen and put on a pot of water. It became a tradition of theirs, Pierre and Dad, and it was a nice moment for Benjamin as well because it made him feel calm, it was bright and let you breathe easy.

The hens stopped pecking at the ground and gazed with their dead eyes at the brothers on the shore. Benjamin lunged at them and the Larsson Sisters immediately picked up the pace, moving on with long steps, staring down into the grass. They passed the boys and were gone.

Pierre was holding the rod when the bobber began to move.

First there was a little tremor, and then it vanished completely into the black water.

"We've got a bite!" Pierre shrieked. "Take it!" he cried, handing the rod to Benjamin.

Benjamin did as his father had taught him—he didn't lift the fish out right away, but reeled it in gently. Benjamin was tugging in one direction and the fish in another, with a strength that took Benjamin by surprise. When he saw the shape of the beast just beneath the surface, saw it struggling wildly to get loose, he cried, "Quick, a bucket!"

Pierre looked around, not sure what to do. "A bucket?" he asked.

"Nils!" Benjamin called. "We've got a fish, bring a bucket!"

He saw movement from the hammock. Nils hurried to the house, then ran down to the lake with a red bucket in hand. Benjamin didn't want to pull too hard for fear that the line might break, but he had to resist as the fish aimed for the center of the lake. Nils didn't hesitate; he stepped into the water and sank the bucket.

"Pull it in!" he cried.

The fish slapped at the surface, moving closer to land again. Nils took another step into the water, his shorts got wet, and he scooped up the fish.

"I've got it!" he shouted.

They gathered around the bucket and looked inside. "What is it?" Pierre asked.

"A perch," Nils replied. "But you have to toss it back."

"Why?" Pierre asked, surprised.

"It's too small," he said. "You can't eat that."

Benjamin gazed into the bucket and saw that the fish was

flailing against the sides. It was smaller than he'd expected while he was fighting it in the water. Its comb-shaped scales glittered; its sharp dorsal fins bristled.

"Are you sure?" Benjamin asked.

Nils chuckled. "Dad will laugh in your faces if you show him that."

Pierre picked up the bucket and marched toward the house. Benjamin followed close behind.

"What are you doing? You have to put it back in the water," Nils cried. When they didn't respond, he ran to catch up with them.

Pierre set the bucket on the kitchen table. He looked down at the fish, and the red plastic of the bucket was reflected on Pierre's face, making it look like he was blushing.

"Shall we fry it alive?" he asked softly. Nils stared at his brother in shock.

"You're not fucking right in the head," he said.

He turned around and went outside, and Benjamin heard him say, as he passed by the window, "Madhouse."

Benjamin watched him go, saw him lie down in the hammock. "Let's fry it alive," Pierre said again, looking at Benjamin.

"No," said Benjamin. "We can't do that." Pierre stood on a chair and took down one of the frying pans that hung on the wall over the counter. He set it on the gas stove and stared at the knobs in confusion. He turned one and suddenly they could hear the gentle whisper of the gas. He leaned forward, looking down along the burners.

"How do you light it?" he asked. He twisted the knob back and forth but only heard the gas starting and stopping. He turned to Benjamin.

"Come on, help me!"

"You need matches," Benjamin told him.

"So can you help me or what?"

"Pierre," said Benjamin. "You can't fry a fish that's alive."

"Stop it," said Pierre. "Just help me."

And the gas trickled into the room, and a window slammed upstairs, and the swallows that had built nests in the ridge of the roof scraped at the wood as if they were scratching the house, and the afternoon sun shone in onto the rough planks of the kitchen table, onto the yellowed deck of cards that was still there from their parents' games the night before, sunshine from the side onto the two brothers, illuminating the dead flies that lay in little drifts on the windowsill, and Benjamin looked out the window and then back at Pierre. And then he took the matches from the top drawer and struck one against the burner which immediately flared up with red flames.

"Do we need butter or something?" Pierre asked, looking around the room. Benjamin didn't answer. Pierre dug around in the fridge but didn't find what he was looking for. He came back to the stove; it smoked a little as the fire heated the pan. Pierre lifted the red bucket and dumped the fish into the frying pan. It tumbled out and threw itself violently into the air when it touched the iron. Then its strength was sapped. It stuck to the pan, its gills heaving, careful movements from its tail. It tried once or twice to pull loose, but its scales had begun to melt and it was slowly riveted to the iron.

The pan began to smoke. Benjamin, speechless, looked on. Pierre tried to work a spatula gently under the fish to turn it. He poked and prodded and squinted when the smoke got into his eyes, and eventually he pried it loose. The place where it had just been was covered in scales. The fish threw itself into the air, tried to flip over, and landed in the same spot. Both brothers leapt back and stared at the pan.

"It's still alive!" Benjamin said. "We have to kill it!"

"You do it, I'm scared," Pierre said.

"Why me?" Benjamin hissed.

Pierre shoved Benjamin, trying to push him toward the pan. "Stop it!"

The fish flipped over again.

"You're the one that did this!" said Benjamin.

Pierre was frozen, staring at the pan with his mouth open. Benjamin hurried to the stove and turned the knob, setting the gas to max. He backed away, recoiling, and stood beside his brother. Through the smoke they heard small noises, the fish slapping its tail against the pan; it was as though it were keeping time against the iron as the heat got worse. Benjamin felt like his legs were about to give out and grabbed the arm of a chair to steady himself. There was a sudden sizzling sound as the fish burst and its innards slipped into the pan; the smoke thickened and there was something about this experience that made Benjamin feel that God was involved, when the smoke was lit by the sun as it rose to the ceiling, and he thought that the pillar of smoke created a canal, a divine channel, that through it the fish was rising to heaven. And suddenly everything was crystal clear, as if all the events on earth had suddenly concentrated into this frying pan, the weight of the planet exerting all its pressure there on the gas range.

Then it was over. Everything was still.

Benjamin went over to the pan and put it in the sink. He ran water into it; the sizzling was replaced with a different kind of sizzling, and then it was quiet. He looked at the charred little fish, which still lay in the pan. He scooped it into the trash and put some paper on top of it. He walked over to Pierre, who was still standing motionless a few steps from the stove.

"This was wrong, Pierre."

Pierre gazed seriously up at his brother.

"Get lost and I'll take care of this," said Benjamin.

Pierre vanished, Benjamin watching through the window as he ran full speed for the barn. Benjamin washed the frying pan, scraping under hot water to get all the fish scales off.

He went out to the stone steps. It was so bright out that everything looked black. He heard vague sounds from inside the house, someone on the stairs, and suddenly there stood the dog, just up from an afternoon nap.

"Hey there, hi there," Benjamin whispered, using his mother's typical call for the dog, and he patted his knee and Molly hopped into his arms, settling into place there. He held her; maybe his heart would stop beating so fast if he pressed her warm body to his chest. He stood up, took the path to the lake, and sat on one of the big rocks with Molly. It was still like an eclipse out there, and as the colors returned he could see clearly what he had suspected: the world had changed. He saw the ripples on the water left by a school of fish fighting for food under the surface. He saw the rings on the water, noticed they were moving not out but in. The rings shrank toward the center and vanished without a trace into their own ripples. He stared out at the bay and saw the same phenomenon again. The rings on the lake sought their own center, as if someone were playing a movie backward. He was startled by the echo of a scream over the lake. He looked out, trying to locate the source. Then he screamed. He realized that time hadn't stopped at all—it was moving backward.

He covered his eyes with his palms.

"Hey there, hi there!"

Who was that? Through his fingers he glanced up at the darkened lawn and saw Mom and Dad, newly awakened and dazed. Mom had spotted the dog in Benjamin's arms and called for her. And slowly the world straightened out again.

He released Molly, who dashed to Mom, and Benjamin ran along the trampled path after her. His parents were staring down at the grass. Mom took out a pack of cigarettes and placed it on the table, reached for the dog.

"Hello, son," Dad said in a thick voice.

"Hi," said Benjamin.

He sat down on the grass. Silence. Mom glanced his way. "Come scratch my back," she said.

Benjamin went to stand behind her, scratched carefully, and Mom closed her eyes and made a small sound, his hand inside her shirt. "Hold on," she said, unclasping her bra so he could reach better.

He felt the impressions on her skin from the band as he ran his fingers from the back of her neck and down over her shoulder blades. And he scratched deliberately, just the way he knew she liked, because he didn't want the moment to end. Mom cast a quick glance up at Benjamin.

"Why are you crying, honey?"

Benjamin didn't respond, just kept scratching his mother.

"What's wrong?"

"Nothing," he said.

"Sweetie," Mom said. "Don't cry." Then she fell silent, bowed her head. "A little farther down."

From the corner of his eye Benjamin saw the Larsson Sisters sneaking up to the patio. They lined up on the lawn, observing what was going on. He felt his heart beating. He thought of the fish, of the smoking frying pan, the scales sticking to the iron. The hens stared at him. They knew what he had done and were judging him in silence.

And he scratched his mother as he looked at the hens, afraid to look away, afraid to look up. He didn't dare to aim his gaze at the table, because he was afraid he would find lunch still on it, the meal just ended, and Mom and Dad about to take a siesta.

| 5 |

Benjamin stands down by the lake with a bouquet of dried buttercups in his hand. His brothers stand beside him. Nils is holding the urn. It's heavy, and he constantly adjusts his grip on it, an increasingly baffled expression on his face, as if the weight of Mom has taken him by surprise.

"Should we say something," Nils says, "or what do we do?"

"I don't know," Benjamin says.

"A ceremony or something?"

"I guess we should just start."

"Hold on," says Pierre. "I have to pee."

He takes a few steps away, faces the water, and unzips his fly.

"Please," Nils says. "Can't this be a solemn occasion?"

"Absolutely. But I have to pee."

Benjamin considers Pierre's back, listens to the urine splashing against the stones at the water's edge. He watches as Nils adjusts his grip on the urn.

"Do you need a hand? Should I hold on to that for a while?"

Nils shakes his head.

The lake is calm and Benjamin can see the forest turned upside down on it, and he sees two skies, both shimmering pink and yellow. In the distance, the sun sinks below the colossal fir trees. Out in the cove, a Styrofoam buoy rests in the still water.

"Look," Benjamin says, pointing at the buoy. "Isn't that ours?"

Nils cautiously scratches at a mosquito bite on his forehead and gazes at the little dot out there.

"No fucking way," he says. "Those last days we were here. Did we put in the net the day before it all happened? And then it was chaos, and when we went home we were suddenly in such a hurry. Did we really . . . ?"

He laughs.

"Did we really forget to bring up the net before we left?"

Benjamin looks at the buoy, a good distance out, but not so far that he can't make out its shape—it's gnawed at the edges, from the winter when rats ruled the boathouse.

"Are you saying it's been there this whole time?" Benjamin asks.

"Yes."

Benjamin pictures the net. At a depth of fifteen feet, a floating mass grave, fish hanging side by side in various stages of decay. Scales and bones, and eyes gazing into the darkness, everything caught in the thin, algae-covered mesh, and the years pass and things happen up there, families pack up and vanish, and everything stands empty, seasons change and decades go by, everything in a constant flux, but fifteen feet down the net is still there, waiting patiently, embracing those that come near.

"Maybe we should bring it up," Nils says.

"Yes," says Benjamin.

"Sometime tomorrow maybe, before we go home."

Pierre, a few steps away, lets out a shrill sound, an excited little screech, as if he wants to object but hasn't found the words to do so yet, even as he's taking measures to get rid of the last drops, his back to his brothers.

"Hell no," he cries. He zips his fly. "Let's do it now!"

"But we're having a ceremony right now," Nils says.

"It can wait," Pierre says. "The brothers back in the boat, out on the lake. One last trip, in the sunset. Mom would have liked that!"

"No, not right now," Nils says, but Pierre is already walking along the embankment, jumping from rock to big rock along the shore. "Think the boat's still there?" he calls. Benjamin and Nils exchange quick glances. Nils smiles his gentle smile. They follow their little brother to the boathouse.

Yes, the boat is still there. Carefully pulled up onto the thick blocks, the old white fiberglass boat, just as they left it. Moss has grown over parts of the floor and the seats in the bow, and the water that's gathered in the stern has created its own ecosystem of algae and slime, but the boat is intact. The oars are hidden on the floor under a tarp as usual, and the brothers position themselves on either side of the boat; Pierre, project manager of their expedition, calls out "Now" and they pull, and rocks clatter under the hull until it slips into the dark water and the lake is dead silent again.

Benjamin rows and Pierre and Nils sit in the stern, making the boat back-heavy—the bow points into the sky. It's so immediately familiar. Benjamin looks at his brothers. They're wearing black suits and ties, to honor Mom. Pierre is wearing sunglasses that seem too big and strangely feminine to Benjamin. Nils has taken off his shoes and socks and rolled up his pant legs to keep from getting them wet. They don't speak, just listen to the gentle slap of the oars, the drops scattering across the surface as Benjamin lifts them alongside the boat. Dusk is falling fast, the shore grows milky, Benjamin looks up and outer space is suddenly there although the sky is still light. He looks at the cottage above the embankment, the door wide open, as if Mom and Dad are about to come out, walk down to the lake with their little basket full of drinks and sausage. He sees the grassy field where he once played soccer with his brothers; it's now overgrown with wildflowers. A cold breeze blows across the water.

"Hey," Pierre calls. They're almost to the buoy and the brothers get ready, as they always did when they were children, turning around in their assigned positions, and Benjamin backs the boat up the last little bit and Nils bends down and captures the buoy.

"We should be prepared to see some pretty nasty things," Nils says.

Then he begins to haul in the discolored yellow nylon line, gathering it into the boat. The first lengths are easy, but then comes the weight of the net. He's not prepared for the resistance, loses his balance in the boat and has to sit down.

"Jesus," he mutters. "Pierre, help me pull it in."

Pierre and Nils stand on unsteady legs and work together and the net moves, slowly approaching the surface of the water.

"I can see the net shuttle!" Pierre calls. And Benjamin stands up and sees the shape of the net with all its hidden cargo, like a darkness traveling through an even bigger darkness, and the brothers tug and grimace as the nylon cuts into their hands, and just when the net reaches the surface the line breaks. The boat sways, the brothers grab on to the sides, look over the railing, see the colossus vanishing back into the depths.

Pierre laughs, howling across the lake. Nils looks at his brother with a smile. He starts to laugh, and it spreads to Benjamin too; now all three of them are laughing. Benjamin turns the boat and begins to row back to land.

Mom wrote, in the letter the brothers found in her apartment, that she wanted her ashes to be scattered in the lake at the cottage. She didn't say exactly where, but the brothers agree they've found the right spot. She used to like to sit and read the morning paper at the edge of the water, on the farthest tip of the point. And she sat there at night, too, just before the sun went down, when the light turned golden, and listened to the wind rustling through the trees, wandering from treetops in the distance to treetops close by, its sounds shifting depending on which kind of tree it touched. And no matter how windy it was during the day, the same thing always happened—just as the sun set, the wind would die down and the lake would grow still. Now the brothers are lining up there, at that very moment, at the water's edge. Nils is carrying the urn, and he stands in front of his brothers.

"I wonder if I need to pee," Pierre says.

"Again?" Nils says.

"Yes?"

"Oh my God," Nils mumbles.

"It's no fun to pee your pants, right?"

"No," Nils says. "Not like it hasn't happened before."

"True," says Pierre.

"In that sense, you're the winner," Nils says, grinning. "Most pants peed as a child."

"I was a joyful kid, I was always busy, and it was such a pain to go to the bathroom."

The three brothers laugh, the same laugh, it sounds like someone crumpling up a piece of newspaper.

"One time in second grade I peed my pants when we were playing soccer during recess," Pierre says. "Just a few drops, but enough to soak through my jeans. A dark spot the size of a coin, right on my fly. Björn noticed that pretty quick."

"I remember Björn," Benjamin says. "He was always good at finding someone's weak point."

"Right. He saw the spot and started pointing and shouting. Everyone was looking at me. But I told them a ball had hit me right there. Because it had just been raining, and the field was wet, and the ball too, so it was a perfectly reasonable explanation. Björn shut up about it and we kept playing. I was pretty happy, because that wasn't such a bad lie. It was genius. Peed my pants and got away with it."

His brothers laugh.

"But then more pee came out," Pierre says. "The spot got

bigger. And Björn was back on the case. When recess was over and we were all heading inside, he walked next to me, staring. He kept looking down at my pants. When we got to the classroom, he shouted, 'Pig pile on Pierre!'"

"Pig pile?" Benjamin asked.

"Yeah. Didn't you ever get piled on? It's when someone shouts a name and everyone has to lie on top of them in one big pile."

"So then what happened?" Benjamin asked.

"Everyone jumped on me. And I was at the very bottom and couldn't move. Björn was right on top of me. He was lying there with his head next to mine, so we were face-to-face, and I remember he was grinning at me. Then he shoved his hand into my jeans. I tried to stop him, but I was completely stuck. He dug around in my wet underwear and pulled out his hand and smelled it. He screamed, 'It's piss! Pierre pissed himself!'"

Benjamin shakes his head.

"Weren't there any teachers around?" he asks.

"I don't remember," Pierre responds. "None who intervened, at least."

Pierre picks up a rock from the shore and throws it into the water.

"They were lying there on top of me and everyone started screaming that I'd pissed myself."

Benjamin notices that red spots have appeared on Pierre's neck. He's familiar with those spots; when they were kids he always saw them when Pierre was scared or angry.

"While I was lying there I could see out to the hallway," Pierre says. "And I saw you standing there watching from the doorway."

Pierre turns to Nils, quietly nailing him with his gaze. "Nope," Nils says. "Never happened."

"Yeah it did," Pierre says. "You saw me lying there. And then you just walked away."

Nils quickly shakes his head; Benjamin recognizes his nervous, tense smile.

"Say whatever you want," Pierre says. "It's crystal clear in my memory, and I'll never forget it. I didn't think too much about it back then. It wasn't until later on that it blew my mind. You were so much older. It would have been so simple for you to come in and put a stop to what they were doing to me."

Pierre looks at Nils.

"But you just walked away," Pierre says.

Nils looks at the urn in his arms. He rubs his thumb over the lid as if he is trying to get rid of a speck of dirt.

"I don't know what you're talking about," he says.

"Maybe you don't remember?" Pierre asks. "That was often the case. You never saw anything, never heard anything. As soon as things went off the rails, you shouted that you lived in a madhouse, and then you closed yourself up in your room. But just because you didn't see it didn't mean it was any less of a madhouse on the other side of your door."

"Take off your sunglasses," Nils says, his tone suddenly sharp. "Show some respect for Mom, quit your act."

"I'll do whatever the fuck I want," Pierre responds.

Benjamin dials in his focus. He can feel the conversation starting to turn; he can see it in the way Nils's grip on the urn hardens, how he doesn't take his eyes off Pierre.

"You'd better listen up, because I'm only going to say this

once," Nils says. "I don't want to hear another word about how badly treated you were when we were kids. Not another word."

"You failed me," Pierre says. Nils stares at Pierre.

"I failed you?" he says. He laughs suddenly. "You think we should feel sorry for you? I can't remember a single day when you and Benjamin didn't harass me when we were kids. You made me feel worthless. And now we're supposed to feel sorry for you?"

Pierre gazes at the lake, shaking his head.

"Let's just do this thing, and you can cry afterward."

Nils takes a step toward Pierre, coming up right beside him. "Don't you fucking trivialize it."

Pierre's reaction is immediate; he mirrors Nils's step forward. Benjamin approaches in a baffled attempt to get between them. Now all three of them are standing close, in a web of aggression that is completely foreign to them. Suddenly there is no rage in their eyes, only confusion. They exchange nervous glances. They have no idea what they're doing.

"Let's calm down," Benjamin says.

"I'm not going to calm down," says Nils. "You think I checked out when we were kids? Well, is it any wonder that I didn't want to be there, when I got called ugly and disgusting every time I showed my face? And you would do that thing with your eyes."

"What thing?" Pierre asks. He doesn't say anything for a moment. Then he crosses his eyes, imitating Nils with a grin.

Nils shoves the urn with full force at his brother. Pierre isn't ready for it and it lands on his chest. From the crack, Benjamin knows immediately that something has broken inside Pierre's body.

6

KINGS OF THE BIRCH

Dinner on the patio, just before everyone scatters. Mom took out a cigarette and moved around empty bowls to find the lighter. Dad gazed anxiously at his empty plate, not quite satisfied. Mom had cut the rind off her ham steak, and now Dad was eyeing it. He kept sneaking looks at it, the strip of fat like a charred finger on her plate, sizing it up from the corner of his eye, deliberating.

"That right there . . . ," he said at last, pointing at the leftover fat.

Mom quickly stuck a fork in it and transferred it to Dad's plate. "Thanks," Dad muttered, attacking it. Mom watched him as he ate. Tiny signs of disgust on her face; Benjamin the only one who could see them. He knew all about Mom's annoyance at Dad's boundless appetite; she hated it when his eyes roamed other people's plates, when he snuck into the kitchen after dinner to make a "reinforcement sandwich," when he stood gazing listlessly into the fridge in the afternoon, on the hunt for something to stuff in his mouth. Sometimes Mom exploded, accusing him of being an animal. Usually Dad's response was silence—he would quickly close the fridge door and walk off—but sometimes he reacted with an equal amount of rage: "Let me eat!"

Dad put down his flatware and pounded his fist on the table. "Boys!" He wiped his mouth with a wad of paper towel. "I thought I would show you a place none of you has seen before. Who wants to come?"

Benjamin and Pierre stood up right away. The cottage was the cottage and the cottage was the world. It was the small buildings surrounded on all sides by forest and water. Everything else was uncharted territory—the point of land like a glowing, pulsing green dot on an otherwise gray map of the world. If Dad said he would show them a new place, it amounted to a promise to make the known world greater. They prepared as if for a difficult expedition. Dad put on his tall boots, which came up to his knees, and ordered Benjamin and Pierre to put on their caps as gnat protection.

"Are you coming, Nils?" Dad asked.

"No," he replied.

"It's a secret place," Dad said. "A place where children can become rich."

"No," said Nils, reaching for his milk glass, drinking what was left in the bottom. "I don't feel like it."

They walked down the slope, across the meadow. Dad reached down and let the tall grass slip through his fingers;

he picked a piece of straw and stuck it between his teeth. He pressed on confidently. Benjamin and Pierre followed, swept along in his wake, sometimes glancing past Dad's back to see where they were going. They walked in among the trees. All of a sudden it was dark.

"Are you still afraid of the forest, Benjamin?" Dad asked.

"No, not really," Benjamin replied.

"During our first summer here you always started crying when we walked in the forest," Dad said. "I don't know why—you wouldn't tell us."

"No," Benjamin said. He couldn't put it into words, but the unsettled feeling the forest gave him had been there for a long time, especially after a rain, when the trees were heavy and the bogs were spongy. It was a fear of getting stuck there, being sucked in and vanishing.

"There's one thing I know about forests," Dad said. "And that's that everyone has a forest that is theirs alone. They know it inside and out and it makes them safe. And having your own forest is the best thing there is. All you have to do is hike around enough here, and soon you'll know every rock, every tricky trail, every fallen birch. And then the forest will be yours, it will belong to you."

Benjamin gazed into the dark abyss. It didn't feel like his. "Come on, let's get moving," Dad said. "We're almost there."

They passed the dam that controlled the flow between lake and river—neither Benjamin nor Pierre had been so far from the house before. From here on, everything was new and unexplored. They passed a swamp with large stones rising from the peat, walked through the spruce forest, and suddenly a clearing appeared. Dad bent back a spruce bough and allowed them to walk on ahead.

"Welcome to my secret place!"

A dense group of young birches rose in front of them, forming their own little forest. Thin, fragile, close together, like rust-bitten lampposts, and the lake glittered between their trunks.

"What do you think?" Dad asked.

"Pretty!" Benjamin said. He didn't want to show his disappointment. They were only trees.

"How many are there?" Pierre asked.

"I don't know," Dad replied. "Several hundred."

"That's so many," Pierre said.

"Just think, that this happened to us," Dad said, "that these trees are right here. They're very rare. There are plenty of birches in Sweden—warty birch, pyramid birch, weeping birch, all kinds. But these, boys, are silver birch." He laid a hand on one trunk and gazed up. "The finest birches of all. Nothing on earth can beat the scent of silver birch in the sauna."

Benjamin walked up and touched one of the trees. He grabbed a twig and tried to break it loose from the tree, but it didn't want to let go.

"I'll show you how to do it," Dad said. "Never pull on the twig, just snap it. And snap it close to the base, because you need something to hold on to so you don't get too close to the hot stones when you throw on the water."

Benjamin watched as his dad harvested twig after twig and gathered up his bouquet of birch in his left hand. It looked so simple. "Don't just stand there," Dad said to the boys with a smile. "Help me."

They stood side by side, in lighthearted silence. For a brief moment Dad gazed into the forest and muttered "Cuckoo" after a bird called, but otherwise they were quiet, absorbed in their task.

"Do you know why they're called silver birch?" Dad asked.

"No."

"It's a strange name, isn't it? There's nothing about them that's silver. The leaves are green and the trunks are gray. But they say something happens to them at night."

He crouched down and gazed up at the treetops. "When the full moon shines down on them, they change color. If you look closely, you'll see that the leaves are made of silver."

"Is that true?" Pierre asked.

"Yes."

Pierre stared wide-eyed at Dad.

"Stop," Benjamin said and turned to his brother. "Of course it isn't true."

Dad laughed and ruffled Pierre's hair. "But it's a pretty nice story, isn't it?"

They snapped and gathered as the sun fell behind the trunks. Pierre took off his cap, waving gnats away, and scratched his whole head violently. Dad was finished first.

"Something like that," he said, taking in his birch whisk with satisfaction. "I need ten whisks that I'll hang to dry on the porch to the sauna. For if we ever come here in the winter, when there are no leaves on the trees. I'll give you five kronor for each whisk you make."

Benjamin and Pierre exchanged a determined high five, already intent on their assignment, ready to work for the money.

"I'm going to head back and have a drink with Mom," Dad said. "Come back as soon as you've got something to show me."

And he vanished back toward the house.

Benjamin began to snap twigs and gather up the first whisk. He tried to calculate how much money they actually stood to earn. Ten whisks would be fifty kronor, divided by two. And then he converted the money to gum, fifty öre per piece, which would give him fifty pieces of gum, and if he chewed one piece a day it would last the whole summer. He had learned to use his gum sparingly. One night he'd stuck his used gum on the nightstand when he went to bed, and when he woke up he had the sudden urge to stick it in his mouth again. He found that it had regained its flavor, that it was like a fresh piece, more or less. It was as if he had gamed the system. This discovery changed everything—he began to reuse his gum, and one piece suddenly lasted several days. But then he got careless and left chewed pieces where Mom could find them, and she forbade all such activity.

He was finished with his first whisk and looked down at Pierre, who stood next to him empty-handed, his lower lip trembling.

"I can't do it," he said. "I can't snap the twigs."

"It's no big deal. I'll pick yours too."

"But . . . ," Pierre said. "Will I still get the money?"

"Sure. We'll share."

Benjamin picked another ten twigs and handed them to Pierre. "Let's run back and show Dad."

They ran through the twilight with the birch whisks in hand, dodging between the spruce trees and past the dam and out to the meadow below the house, and there, at the foot of the stone steps, they could see Mom and Dad at the table, like a little glowing island of candles in the dim evening light. Another bottle of wine on the table. Dad had brought out a sausage. They placed the whisks in Dad's lap.

"Bravo!" Dad said.

"What a thing," said Mom.

Dad inspected the whisks carefully, as if he were doing quality control. He had placed a stack of five-kronor coins on the table, and a shiver went through Benjamin as he noticed the shiny pile. Dad took two coins and ceremoniously handed one to each boy.

"Are you going to be birch harvesters when you grow up?" Mom asked.

"Maybe," Pierre replied.

"Maybe," Mom repeated with a smile.

Mom reached out to the boys. "My darlings," she said, and they hugged. "You're so sweet, doing things together." Her chilly cheek against Benjamin's hot one. She smelled like mosquito repellant and cigarettes. She pressed the boys' heads to her breast and ran her fingers through their hair, and when she let go they were dazed, as if they'd just woken up; they stood there, at a loss, and looked at Mom's smile.

"The children's first summer job," Dad said, and suddenly his eyes filled with tears. The flames of the candles flashed in his eyes. "It's beautiful," he mumbled, searching his pocket for his handkerchief. Mom gave him her hand.

"Off with you, boys," Dad cried, and the brothers dashed away. "Go get more," he called after them, but by then the boys were already halfway across the meadow, running on their nimble, nimble legs in the summer night. And it went quickly now—Benjamin didn't even have to look after he snapped the twigs, just handed them over blindly and there stood Pierre to gather them up, and when they had two more whisks they ran back the same way they'd come, their sights trained on the little vessel of light in the yard. Dad called to them from a distance: "They've done it again!" The boys ran faster, the drumming of their feet against the dirt path to the garden. "The boys have done it again!"

Dad took the whisks and inspected them, then looked up at the children. "You're kings of the birch."

And they ran back out again. Darkness was falling swiftly, the path through the forest was harder to see, twigs melting into the dim light struck their faces. When they arrived, the lake beyond the birches was a pale gray streak.

"Want to skip rocks?" Pierre asked.

They walked through the silver birches, down to the lake, grabbing each tree they passed to make them rattle together. They searched the shore for suitable rocks. Pierre tossed one and there was a commotion where it landed, fish just below the surface quickly revealing themselves before vanishing into the depths.

"Hello!" Pierre called across the lake, and the echo bounced off the tall trees on the other side and came back.

"Hello there!" Benjamin and Pierre called, giggling.

"Kings of the birch!" Pierre cried at the top of his lungs, and the forest confirmed it, calling back that what he'd said was true.

A light fog had formed, so they could no longer see to the

other side. Pierre kicked at the rocks, slapped a mosquito on his arm.

"Are you okay?" Benjamin asked.

"Yeah," Pierre said, looking at him curiously.

Benjamin didn't know what to say, didn't even know what he was trying to say with his question.

"Want to keep gathering?" Benjamin said.

"Yeah. Can you pick for me again?"

"Of course."

And soon they came running back across the meadow, waving the whisks over their heads. Dad was alone at the table.

"Where's Mom?"

"She's just peeing," Dad told him, and Benjamin's eyes searched the shadows behind the lilac bush, Mom's toilet when she didn't feel like going inside, and there she crouched, her pants around her ankles, gazing at the lake.

"Let's see what you've got this time," Dad said, and the boys handed over their whisks. "They're very nice," he said, inspecting them closely. "Tomorrow I'll teach you how to tie a whisk, because it's important—it has to be knotted the right way, if it's going to hang outside and survive the autumn winds."

"So how's it going?" Mom asked as she emerged from the dim foliage.

"The children have produced two more whisks," said Dad.

"I see," Mom said as she sat down. She reached for the bottle of wine and refilled her glass. She looked at the whisks in Dad's lap, then picked one up and weighed it in her hand.

"What's this?" she asked.

Her voice changed; her tone grew sharp.

"The whisks are getting smaller and smaller. Look at this."

She held one up toward the boys. "It's half the size of the first ones you brought."

"It is?" Benjamin asked.

"Don't even try," Mom snapped. "You know exactly what you're doing, don't you?"

"What do you mean?" Benjamin asked.

"You just want the money," she said. "You want to cheat."

"Please," Dad said in English, their code language when he wanted to speak privately to Mom. "Calm down."

"Don't tell me to calm down," said Mom. "This is damn horrible!"

She looked at the children.

"You want money?" She picked up the stack of five-kronor coins, snatched Pierre's hand, and slapped them into his palm.

"Fine. Here. Take it all."

She stood up, grabbing her cigarettes and lighter. "I'm going to bed."

"Honey!" Dad cried after her as she vanished into the house. "Come back, please!"

Pierre rushed to put the money back on the table. Dad remained in his chair, his eyes riveted to the tabletop. The whisk lay on the ground at the brothers' feet.

"We didn't mean to make it smaller," Benjamin said.

"I know," said Dad.

He stood up and blew out candle after candle, and as darkness fell over the table he moved to stand facing the lake, feet planted wide. Benjamin and Pierre stayed put, motionless.

"I know how you can cheer Mom up again."

Dad turned to the children, knelt beside them, whispering now: "You can pick flowers for her."

Pierre and Benjamin didn't respond.

"What if you put a bouquet outside the bedroom door? She would like that a lot."

"But it's pretty dark out now," said Benjamin.

"It doesn't have to be a large bouquet. Just a small one, for Mom. Can you do that?"

"Yes," Benjamin mumbled.

"Pick buttercups. Mom loves them. Those are the little yellow ones, you know?"

Benjamin and Pierre stood still, watching as Dad used a fork to scrape food from plate to plate, then stacked the dishes and glasses to carry them inside. He looked up at the children, surprised to find them still standing there.

"Go on, my sweets," he whispered.

Benjamin and Pierre walked down to the meadow. There were buttercups everywhere, glowing like dull lanterns in the dusk. There was a chill in the summer night, and the grass was damp. Benjamin crouched down and picked the buttercups, not thinking of Pierre, and after a while he realized that Pierre was on his knees in the middle of the meadow, three buttercups in his hand, crying without making a sound. Benjamin embraced him, pressing Pierre's face to his chest, feeling his little brother's body shake as he held him.

"Go on inside and go to bed," Benjamin whispered. "I can finish picking these."

"No," Pierre said. "Mom wants flowers from both of us."

"I'll pick them for the two of us and we'll say they're from us both."

Pierre ran up the slope in the darkness and Benjamin leaned forward, down to the wet grass so he could see in the dark, close to the ground and the soil and the insects, feeling his breath against the surface. He looked up at the cottage and saw Pierre disappear inside, saw the lights burning in there. The two windows that faced the lake reminded him of eyes, as if the house were watching him as he sat there. Then he looked up at the enormous fir trees and imagined how he would appear from up there, from the point of view of the treetops. The cottage, viewed from above, the old roof, the stones over the root cellar, the currant bushes arranged more symmetrically than they seemed from the ground, the grass like an unfurled carpet leading to the water, and a little dark spot in the meadow, Benjamin himself, doing something inexplicable down there. And beyond that, beyond the pond and the thousands of firs, the enormous field of gray unknown. And Benjamin walked away, letting the buttercups lead the way, stooping toward the edge of the meadow and being sucked into the forest, his eyes on the ground. He picked flowers and didn't think about where they were leading him, and suddenly he was once again at the foot of the massive gathering of young birches on the point. The full moon shone behind their trunks and a breeze came through the darkness, the trees rustled. Benjamin took a step back and when the stand of trees was ignited he had to shield his eyes so he wouldn't be blinded. It was as if a rain of embers were descending over the dark point, as if a wild silver fire were spreading uncontrolled through the trees.

7

6:00 P.M.

Benjamin observes Nils's bare back in the sauna. The collection of moles is still there, like a scattershot of brown dots that landed between his shoulder blades. Nils's constant anxiety about them as a child, always rubbing them with creams and sunscreen. And Mom, frequently admonishing him not to scratch. When Nils was reading on the beach, or lying on his belly to sun himself, Pierre and Benjamin would sneak up from behind and scratch him hard on the back, and Nils would fly into a rage, slugging the air around him in wild fury.

This is the first time Benjamin has seen his brothers naked since they were kids. Pierre's genitals are shaved perfectly smooth. There's not a strand of hair in sight. Benjamin has seen it in porn, but in real life the hairlessness really stands out. He looks down at his own penis, a dead thing, a brown stump of flesh that's sleeping in the hair that surrounds it. But Pierre's penis lies there pulsing on the sauna bench, like a being of its own, a sticky little consciousness. Perhaps Pierre notices that Benjamin is staring, because after some time in the sauna he pulls his towel around his waist.

"I didn't know you had so many tattoos," Benjamin says to Pierre. "I haven't seen some of those."

"No? I've been thinking about having some of them removed."

"Which ones?"

"This one, for instance."

He points at a cartoon fist with the words *Save the people of Borneo*.

"What's happened to the people of Borneo?" Benjamin asks.

"Nothing," Pierre says. "That's why I thought it was funny."

Benjamin laughs. Nils shakes his head with a smile, gazing down at his own feet on the lower bench.

"Once when I was drunk I asked a tattoo artist to do an arrow pointing at my dick and write, *It's not gonna suck itself.*"

All the brothers laugh in tandem, three gentle chuckles that settle into each other. Nils glances at the thermometer on the wall and mutters, "A hundred and ninety-four degrees."

"I need a break," Benjamin says, and he goes outside. He stands on the sauna porch. Hanging on one wall is a line of six dried birch whisks. Benjamin leans against the flaking wooden wall and gazes up at the tidy line. He reaches for the sixth whisk, the one that's a little smaller than the others, and runs his palm gently across the sharp dried leaves.

Nils comes out of the sauna. "Come on, time for a dip!" he

says, running down off the small porch, hopping a bit as he steps on something sharp, stopping at the edge of the water, and as he hesitates he looks as he did as a child, on those summer days when Dad shouted at him from up here, getting more and more upset, yelling at him to jump in, that the water was fine, what was he waiting for, and Dad's voice got shriller and shriller, soon wild with frustration that the boy couldn't just jump in, until at last Nils, furious, walked off without taking a swim. Pierre flings open the door of the sauna and staggers out of the heat, down to the shore. He wades into the water, his arms extended, hissing "Shit" as he steps funny on a rock and almost falls over. And then he dives in and swims off. It looks exquisite: slow strokes straight into the lake. Benjamin goes down to the beach and stands beside Nils. The water is low; they must have opened the dam recently. Among the damp rocks he can see a little perch lying on its side in the wet gravel; it must have been left behind when the water level fell. He bends down and picks the fish up by one fin.

"Look," he says.

He gently places the fish in the water and watches it slowly rotate and end up upside down. It bobs there, with its white belly just at the surface. He gives the fish a little nudge with one finger, trying to straighten it out, but the fish lies on its side for a moment. He watches its gills move, it's not dead, but it doesn't have the strength to right itself and flips upside down again. It was part of him even as a child, his fear of fish. He liked fishing but hated getting a bite. It was something about that unpredictable flopping when a fish took the lure.

The realization that there was a living creature on the other end of the line, something with a consciousness. And when the fish showed itself at the surface, flailing until the water frothed, fighting for its life, Benjamin felt something like an existential disgust. Dad would help kill and clean the fish. Always the same horror when Dad placed the fish upright on the wooden bench and drove a knife through its neck. "Those are just reflexes, kids," he said as it jerked in his grip, and it just kept going, Dad had to press harder with the knife, deeper, as he repeated for the children: "He can't feel anything. He's already dead." On occasion, the fish would twitch for so long that even Dad was alarmed, his eyes darted, he didn't know what to do.

The abrupt shifts from barbarism to finesse as he worked with the fish. How he so brutally tore out the innards and threw them into the lake, and how his hands then worked so precisely, with solemn silence from the children, to pick out the spleen, which could poison the meat of the fish if it burst.

Benjamin crouches in the shallow water, poking at the fish again.

And once more.

"Come on, little fish," he whispers. "I'll fight for you."

Now it's upright, sensitive to the current of the water, but it can manage, it holds still for a little while. Orienting itself in the lake. And then, suddenly, it swims off and is gone.

He looks at his brother.

"Well," Benjamin says. "Just have to do it."

"I suppose," Nils says.

And they swim out on their sides, like old men, a few splashes of their feet and they get up, stand beside each other, all three together. The water's warm enough that they can stay put, linger for a moment, without any pain.

"Should we do another round in the sauna?" Nils asks.

"Definitely," Pierre says. "Just need to empty my bowels in the lake first."

"Jesus Christ," Nils mutters, wading back to land.

Pierre's laugh echoes across the lake. "Come on, I was just kidding!"

They cram into the sauna again, gazing out through the little windowpane that faces the water.

"Didn't we bury that time capsule somewhere around here?" Pierre asks.

Benjamin stands up and looks out. "Yeah. Right by that tree, I think."

He remembers the old metal bread box their dad gave them, and how Benjamin and Pierre filled it with artifacts and buried it deep in the ground. It was a scientific project that involved preserving important information for posterity, to show how people lived in the twentieth century.

"We need to find it," Pierre says.

"I think that might be hard," Benjamin replies.

"Why? All we have to do is dig, right?"

"But we don't know exactly where we buried it."

"Stop," Pierre says. "I'm going to find it!"

He dashes out of the sauna and the brothers watch through the window as he reaches the little patch outside. He falls to his knees by the tree and frantically begins to dig in the ground with his hands. He brings up some soil and scoops it aside and tries again, but it immediately becomes clear that this won't work; he's digging but can hardly get past the first layer of soil. He kneels on the ground for a moment, at a loss. Then he gets up and dashes off, up to the barn.

"What is he doing?" Nils says.

"He's sick," Benjamin responds.

Nils reaches for the bucket and tosses water on the rocks, and the unit hisses. Benjamin watches as beads of sweat form on his chest.

"How do you feel, being here?" Nils asks.

"I don't know," Benjamin replies. "It's like part of me is telling me I'm home. A different part is shouting at me that I have to get out of here."

Nils chuckles. "Same."

"It was weird to see this place again," Benjamin says. "I've been here so many times in my mind. Falling through the events, over and over. And now . . ."

He looks out the window.

"It was just strange," Benjamin says.

"Benjamin," Nils says. "I'm so sorry, for everything."

They gaze at each other and quickly lower their eyes again. Nils tosses more water on the rocks, which swiftly shush them, ask them to be quiet.

Pierre reappears outside the window, with clogs on his feet and a shovel in his hands. He peers at the sauna window and waves wildly above his head. He pushes the shovel into the ground, hard, causing his penis to hop and then fall back against his thigh. And he begins to dig. He's sweaty and determined, grunting with each thrust of his foot against the shovel, amplifying them into loud groans.

"He'll never find it," Benjamin mutters.

The sound of the shovel against metal can be heard all the way into the sauna. Benjamin and Nils lean toward the window. Pierre throws himself to the ground and begins to dig with his hands. He lifts something from the hole and Benjamin recognizes it right away. It's covered in soil, but in some spots the rusty metal gleams—it's the bread box. Pierre stands up straight, his legs planted wide, holding the box above his head and shouting without words, like a barbarian who's just discovered fire. Benjamin and Nils dash out of the sauna. Pierre places the box on the little table on the sauna porch and they gather around.

"Are you ready?" Pierre asks. "Because we're about to pay a visit to ourselves as kids."

He opens the box. At the top is an issue of the morning newspaper. NATO bombings in Sarajevo. Under that is a small envelope. Benjamin opens it and thinks it's empty at first, but then he spots something in the bottom. He pours the contents onto the table—it looks like a bunch of small, plastic half-moons. Benjamin can't tell what they are right away.

But then: "Oh my God."

"What is it?" Nils asks.

Benjamin bends down, poking at the yellowish little pile before him.

"It's our nails."

"What?" Nils says.

"We clipped our nails," he says. "Remember, Pierre?"

Pierre nods as he sits down at the table and pokes cautiously at the tiny little-boy nails. "We did your left hand and my right hand. Ten fingernails, so the future would see who we were."

Benjamin tries to arrange the ten nails in proper order, with the two wider thumbnails in the middle and another four on either side. He places his own hand just below the clippings and sees the contours of himself as a boy.

Pierre takes a ten-kronor bill from the box. "Look at this," he says.

"I stole that from Mom," says Benjamin. "I remember."

Benjamin exchanges quick glances with his brothers. He sets the bill aside. At the bottom of the box is a bouquet of buttercups, exquisitely dried and well-preserved. The yellow petals gleam in the angled sun. Benjamin hands the bouquet to Pierre. He holds it gently, gazing at it. Then he looks away and covers his eyes with one hand.

"Shall we make another attempt to give this bouquet to Mom?" Benjamin says.

They dry off hastily, put their suits on over their damp skin. They follow each other across the meadow and to the water.

Benjamin stands down by the lake with a bouquet of dried buttercups in his hand. His brothers stand beside him. Nils is holding the urn. It's heavy, and he constantly adjusts his grip on it, an increasingly baffled expression on his face, as if the weight of Mom has taken him by surprise.

8

THE ROOT CELLAR

"So fucking nasty," Nils said as he walked past his brothers. "I can't look at that."

"What are you doing?" Dad asked. He was sitting next to them and reading the paper.

"We're clipping our nails!" said Pierre. "We're going to collect them and put them in the time capsule."

"Why would you put fingernails in a time capsule?"

"What if people look totally different in a thousand years? This way they'll be able to see what our nails looked like."

"Smart," said Dad.

It was early morning, the sun was low in the sky and shining from an odd angle, dew still on the grass, flakes of cereal swollen in the sun-warmed milk of their breakfast bowls. The breeze was brisker than usual for so early in the day, and each time a gust came Dad held the morning paper tight and looked up to see what was going on. He was drinking coffee out of a mug that left another brown ring each time he put it down on the morning paper; sometimes he got up to make a trip to the kitchen, where he would cut thick slices of rye and apply such a rich layer of butter you could see the marks left by his teeth when he took a bite. Benjamin and Pierre sat there in their well-worn pajamas, concentrating, clipping their nails and gathering them in a pile on the patio table. When they were done, they put them in an envelope and stuck it in the metal box Dad had given them. The first artifact for their time capsule was secured.

"Dad, can we have today's paper for the time capsule?"

"Of course," Dad said. "As soon as I'm done reading it."

Benjamin observed his father. He was eating two eggs, and Benjamin hoped he'd be done by the time Mom woke up, because she hated to watch Dad eat eggs.

"Do you have any money?" Benjamin asked. "I want to put a bill in the time capsule too."

"Can't you use one of the five-kronor coins you earned yesterday?"

"It has to be a bill, so I can write a greeting on it."

Dad checked his pockets, stood up, and went to the hall to look in his wallet.

"I don't have any money," he called. "You'll have to ask Mom when she wakes up."

"But what are we supposed to do now?" Pierre asked. Always restless.

"Why don't you look for other things to put in your box?" Dad asked.

"There aren't any other things," Pierre replied.

"Then play with Molly," Dad told him.

But that was never really an option for Pierre, or anyone else in the family. Molly wasn't playful. She was anxious, fragile, and easily startled. During the first summer after she came to them, the family thought it would pass, that she needed time to adjust, but by now they understood that she was just like that. It was as if she was afraid of the world, never wanted to be free, preferred to be carried around. She recoiled from Dad and tried to keep her distance from him, despite his awkward attempts to show her tenderness. Neither Nils nor Pierre demonstrated any great interest in her, and maybe there was some jealousy involved, given that it sometimes seemed like Mom showed more care for the dog than for the brothers. Mom's love for Molly was strong but spasmodic, which made Molly even more anxious. Mom sometimes wanted to keep Molly to herself and refused to share her; at other times she was chilly with her. Sometimes Benjamin would find Molly kind of cast off, forgotten as a result of Pierre and Nils's lack of interest, Dad's resignation, and Mom's sudden disengagement.

Benjamin felt a kinship with Molly. They sought each other out, and during the long afternoon hours that summer, when Mom and Dad were having a siesta, they slowly built up their relationship. In secret, Benjamin made her his own. They went down to the lake and threw rocks. They took walks in the forest. They kept each other company.

"Go play with Molly," Dad said.

"But she doesn't want to play with us," said Pierre.

"Sure she does," said Dad. "We just have to give her time."

Pierre trudged off to the barn, where he kept his comic

books, and Benjamin approached the dog and picked her up. He went into the kitchen and sat at the table by the window with Molly in his lap. Outside, the real world shifted as he looked at it through the old glass pane; the foliage wavered as he slowly tilted his head back and forth. There went Dad, along the path by the old barn. Down by the water he saw Nils's hair in the spot on the beach where he liked to sit when he wanted to read in peace. And directly above Benjamin, Mom was sleeping. He was familiar with every step of her awakening, knew what to listen for. Those first, tentative steps as bare feet hit the bedroom floor and, right after that, a sound like whiplash as she pulled up the blind and it hit its own case. A window opened and then came the golden rain outside the kitchen window as she emptied the chamber pot she used when she didn't feel like going downstairs during the night. The little creak as the bedroom door opened, the sudden, quick steps on the stairs, and then she was in the kitchen. He thought about the risks, and the consequences should someone discover him, but there would be plenty of warning signs, plenty of time to flee. He stood up and snuck into the hall, where Mom's purse hung from a hook. He found her wallet and peered down into an adult's universe, so many credit cards in the little slots, receipts and parking slips telling of a rich life, clues to all the great things she was part of when she left her family to go to work. In the billfold were hundred-kronor bills, and fifties and tens, all next to each other. There was an incredible amount of money here. He carefully pulled out a ten, holding it between his thumb and index finger. He reached back toward the purse to return the wallet.

"What are you doing?"

Mom was staring at him from halfway up the stairs. Her

open robe, hair on end, pillow marks on her cheek. He couldn't believe it; it was impossible. How could she suddenly just be there, without any warning at all? It was as if she'd never gone to bed last night, as if she had spent the night on the stairs, sitting there in the darkness and waiting in silence for the dawn, for this moment.

"Answer me, Benjamin. What are you doing?"

"I wanted to borrow a ten from you for a time capsule, but you were sleeping and . . ."

He fell silent. Mom walked down the stairs, took Molly from Benjamin's arms, and placed her gently on the floor. She let her run off before turning to Benjamin. She looked at him for a moment in silence. Her teeth flashed in a quick grimace.

"You don't steal!" she shouted.

"I'm sorry, Mom," he said. "I'm sorry."

"Give me that."

He handed her the bill.

"Let's sit down here for a minute."

She took a seat on the bench in the hall and Benjamin sat down next to her. Two figures suddenly on the other side of the window: his brothers had heard Mom shouting and were here to see what was going on. They pressed their noses to the pane, and Benjamin met their gazes.

He looked out the door, hoping that Dad would come back; he knew it was dangerous when Mom was upset and had him to herself.

"When I was ten, or maybe nine . . . ," Mom said.

She looked up, her eyes searching the ceiling, and she burst out in a little laugh as if she had just thought of an amusing detail in the story she was about to tell.

"I was nine. One day I stole a one-krona coin from my dad's coat pocket. And I hopped on my bike to zoom down to the store because I had decided to buy a lollipop. But halfway there I stopped—out of regret. *What have I done?* I thought. And I stood there for a long time, in anguish. Then I hurried back, and when I got home I snuck into the hall and put the coin back in his coat pocket."

In the silence that followed, Benjamin gazed up at his mother. The story was over, that was clear, but he didn't understand. There was no lesson—it was vague, confusing. What did she mean? Did she want him to put the bill back in her wallet?

"But this . . ." She held the banknote up in front of him. "Stealing money. You just don't do that."

"I'm sorry."

"Why did you do it?"

"Because I knew you wouldn't give me the money."

She looked at him. "Go sit in the root cellar and think about what you've done for a while," she said.

"The root cellar?"

This was a new sort of punishment. In the past he'd always been sent to the sauna, when it wasn't on. And he had to sit there all by himself on the top bench to think about his mistakes. Mom's child-raising methods were strict and rule-based—and, at the same time, inconsistent. Mom was tough but ambiguous. He never knew when his time in the sauna was over, when he was allowed to come out again. He had to figure it out for himself. This meant that he walked around afterward with a lingering guilty conscience, wondering if he had left too soon. But the root cellar was another thing entirely. He hated its cold, damp dark. Those times Dad had asked him to fetch a beer from in there, he'd made sure to keep both the inner and the outer doors wide open, and then took his mark and dashed in, quick into the dark and then out again.

"Can I leave the doors open?" he asked.

"Yes, that's fine," Mom replied.

He stood up right away and walked out; Pierre and Nils looked away as he passed them. He stopped outside the root cellar, his hand on the knob of the rotting door as he gazed up at the wall of trees that rose above him. He turned around and saw Mom watching him from one of the patio chairs. She took out a cigarette and leaned down below the table so she could light it out of the breeze. He walked into the blackness. The cold air struck him. The scent of soil. Once his eyes adjusted, he could see the contours of the room. Against one of the walls was a six-pack of beer and a carton of yogurt. Some junk left over from summers past, a plastic bag and the box from a cake they'd bought for Mom's birthday long ago. In the center of the cellar stood an empty beer crate, which he turned upside down to sit on. He gazed down at his bare feet against the gravelly ground. Watched goose bumps rise on the skin of his thighs. He wished he'd brought a jacket, because he was about to get cold. Through the small doorway he could look out at the summer. He saw the tangle of raspberry bushes and a corner of their soccer pitch, the back of the sauna where the nets were hanging. He saw the dog coming through the tall grass, making her way closer to the opening, stopping at the entrance to peer in.

"Come, Molly," Benjamin whispered.

She took a step into the darkness, trying to see Benjamin.

"Molly," Mom called from the patio. "Come here."

Molly turned to look at Mom and then back to Benjamin.

"Hey there, hi there," Mom called in her singsong. "Come let's have a bite to eat."

The dog ran off and was soon out of sight.

Benjamin watched as a gust of wind suddenly blew across the yard, went through the treetops down by the water and up to the house, and as it reached the root cellar it slammed the door closed. Everything went black. Benjamin shrieked and threw his hands out in front of himself, staggering ahead until he found a wall with his fingertips. He assumed that if he just followed it he would soon reach the door, fumbling along the rough surface, but he seemed only to find deeper darkness and he felt as if he would soon be unable to find his way back. At last he felt a wooden shape, he kicked wildly, and the door flew open. He had made up his mind not to cry, but now he couldn't help it. He wanted out, even though he knew that Mom would only send him right back in. And then there was that feeling of losing his footing, being lifted out of reality. It was happening to him more and more, and he could never predict when it would come. In music class, when they played the drums and the teacher was showing them how to play a cymbal more and more softly, and there was something about that sound slowly fading, how it trickled away from him, a threat that somehow silence could mean the end for him, and he gave a wild scream there in class, woke up in a different place with his parents' faces hovering close above his own.

He looked through the opening to anchor himself with the objects he knew were out there. And maybe it was his emotional state, or the tears, or maybe it was the absolute darkness in here and the absolute brightness out there that made the colors change; they became clearer, more beautiful. As if he were in a dark theater watching an old movie being projected across the doorway to the root cellar. The gray electrical pole turned white before his eyes. The water darkened to raven blue. The lawn glowed, blazing. And there was Dad, coming back from the barn, surrounded by a shimmer, he was like a fairy-tale character, a luminous figure passing by. Dad caught sight of the open cellar door.

"Dammit, what have I told you about this?" he said, heading for the door. "This door must always be kept closed."

"No, don't shut it," Mom said calmly from her chair.

"Why not?" Dad asked.

"Benjamin's in there."

"What do you mean?"

Mom didn't respond. Benjamin watched as Dad peered into the cellar in surprise, then turned back to Mom.

"What's he doing there?"

"He stole money from me."

"He stole money?"

"Yes. So now he has to sit there for a while."

Dad took a step toward the root cellar; now he was right outside. He squinted, trying to see into the dark. Dad was only three yards away but couldn't make him out. Yet Benjamin sat there on his crate, watching Dad and all his colors and contours, watching him light up the whole doorway, an enormous figure surrounded by a wonderful, golden glow. Dad took off his fisherman's cap and scratched his head, standing at the doorway for a moment in thought. He looked over at Mom and back into the darkness. Then he went on his way.

Benjamin doesn't know how long he sat there. One hour? Two? He watched the sun move outside, creating new shadows, watched the clouds come and go. In silence and darkness he saw and heard everything, with superpower hearing; he heard the wind banging at windows, heard the water pump when someone flushed the toilet, heard swallows scraping at wood, and by the time Mom approached the doorway of the root cellar and said he could come out, his ears ached, ringing with sound.

Benjamin walked to the barn, where Pierre was sitting on the floor with his comic books. Pierre looked up at him.

"Hi," he said. "So you're out now? Do you want to finish the time capsule?"

Benjamin nodded.

The brothers passed the patio, where Mom had settled back down with her newspaper.

"You can keep this, by the way," Mom said, pointing, without looking up, at the bouquet of buttercups, which was in a grubby drinking glass on the table.

Benjamin picked up the flowers and the bread box and they went down to the lake. They knelt by the sauna and dug a hole for the time capsule. Dad had recently planted a tree right next to the sauna, so the earth was freshly turned and easy to dig. Pierre helped for a while but got bored when it seemed to take time, so he went to toss rocks into the boathouse, not far off. Benjamin wanted the hole to be deep, so the capsule wouldn't be discovered too early by mistake. He wiped the sweat from his brow and saw Dad coming down the narrow path. Benjamin pretended not to see him and kept digging. He felt Dad's presence as he stood there gazing down at his boy.

"How're you doing, son?"

He didn't respond, stabbing the earth with his trowel, making the hole deeper.

"Are you digging?" Dad asked.

"Yes."

"I have something for your time capsule."

Benjamin looked up. Dad was holding out the ten-kronor bill. "But that's Mom's money."

"We don't need to mention it to her."

Dad crouched down. Benjamin opened the bread box and put the ten inside. Then they covered the hole.

9

4:00 P.M.

They walk in a line back through the forest, heavy steps through the glades where they ran as children. They take it slow on the last little steep bit down the hill, catch themselves among the trees so as not to lose control, and tumble out into the blazing sun. They sit down at the small table just outside the cottage. Pierre walks off and roots through the car for a moment, then returns with a few cans of beer.

"The car stinks like ground beef," he says. "Who the hell brought ground beef?"

"That's the pierogi from Mom's freezer—they thawed out," Nils says. "Want one?"

Pierre laughs, doesn't answer, suppresses some fresh jab. The beer is warm and hisses and foams and the brothers drink it in silence as they gaze at the lake. Benjamin's phone rings, an unknown number; he silences it but lets it keep ringing. It rings again. Benjamin silences it again.

"Aren't you going to answer?" Nils asks.

"Hell no," Benjamin mutters.

A text arrives. Benjamin reads it, first in silence, and then out loud for his brothers:

"'Hi, this is pathologist Johan Farkas. I'm the one who opened up your mother and if you want some information about the cause of death please give me a call.'"

"No, thanks," Pierre says. "Don't want to know."

"Come on," Nils says. "Of course we're going to call back."

Benjamin throws up his hands, indicating that it's up to his brothers to decide what he should do.

"Call him," Nils says.

Benjamin dials the number and places the phone between his brothers on the table. He gives his name and immediately hears a familiar echoey sound on the other end as someone turns off speakerphone and picks up the device, and then there's a voice saying, "Oh, good"—satisfaction that contact has been made.

"Well," says the pathologist, "since the circumstances surrounding your mother's death were a little, uh, how should I put it . . ."

Benjamin hears a distant clatter in the background, as if the pathologist is simultaneously unloading a dishwasher.

"There were some things that weren't clear, so to speak."

"Yes, we were aware of that," Benjamin says.

"Right," the pathologist says absently, and he falls silent;

Benjamin can hear him paging through some documents. "Hold on a second," he says.

Open up. How can you even say that about someone? Benjamin suddenly pictures his mother, opened up. There she lies, on a sterile slab, three levels below the ground in the hospital, cold and alone. His mother's belly like a rose of skin, and hiding somewhere in her viscous innards is the answer to the mystery, jotted down on paper by the pathologist who's leaning over her, information that will be passed on to involved parties, sons who want to know what happened, why it all went so fast, how it was even possible that a person who was planning a trip to the Mediterranean one day was dying an excruciating death the next.

"Well, what baffled us was that events progressed so quickly. So more or less immediately after the death, we decided to take a look and see what happened."

"And what did you find?"

"Your mother had previously had a tumor in her thyroid gland, were you aware of that?"

"Yes," Benjamin said.

"She also had inflammation in her abdominal cavity. We found a perforation in the wall of her stomach, and the stomach acid leaked out, you might say, causing larger and larger portions of her belly to become inflamed. Unfortunately, this is a very painful condition."

The brothers exchange glances around the patio table. Because they were there, they knew what that pain was, they saw it translated onto her face in her last hours of life, how it first appeared as a crook of her eyebrows and on her tense, pursed lips.

Then it got worse. She whimpered and moaned, grabbed at the staff members and snapped cruel things at them. Pressed the button so nurses would appear at the door. When she said her stomach hurt, one nurse asked if she wanted an antacid.

"An antacid?" said Mom. "Do you think this is heartburn or something?" She stared at the nurse, her mouth open, her eyes sparking in contempt. "My stomach is burning! Don't you get it? It's burning like fire!" Even though she was so small and helpless, he felt the terror that came with hearing her voice rise into falsetto, that familiar screeching sound of his childhood, from when she erupted.

She screamed for hours. Then she went silent.

Still entirely conscious, with her eyes fixed on the wall across from her bed, and now she didn't say a word. The brothers tried to reach her, signaling in front of her face, calling her name. But she didn't want to talk anymore. It was like she refused, in protest against her pain.

And then the thing with her face happened. Her mouth must have been dry; her upper lip became stuck to her gums. Her face froze in a grimace, her front teeth creating a sneer that now invaded Benjamin's mind several times a day. That silence was so unlike her. She lived in fury, but her final two hours passed without a sound. She lay there quietly in the bed in the corner of the room, her teeth gleaming in the dim afternoon light. One of the brothers asked a doctor if she was conscious, if she could hear them. After all, her eyes were open. No, the doctors couldn't really say.

At last Mom closed her eyes. More and more people came into the room—as her condition deteriorated—and then, once it was determined that nothing could be done, they trickled back out. The dose of morphine was increased to ease her pain, and maybe that made the end more tolerable for her, but no one was sure because that grimace stayed on her face even as she was rolled out to the chapel, and now that the pathologist is talking about the pain Mom must have felt, it's Mom's silent farewell there in her hospital bed that Benjamin pictures once more. Even as he thanks the pathologist for calling and hangs up, and as the brothers sit without speaking, gazing down at their beer cans, the image pops into his mind. That mute grin, refusing to leave him alone.

"Do you think the sauna is ready?" Pierre asks Benjamin.

"I turned it on an hour ago," Benjamin replies. He looks at the clock. "It should be warm."

Nils hands his phone to Pierre.

"I took a few pictures that actually turned out," Nils says. "Swipe right for more," he says.

On Nils's phone is a photograph of Mom on her deathbed. Pierre groans and hands the phone back to Nils.

"Why do we have to look at that?" Pierre asks.

"I think it's nice," Nils replies. "You can tell she's at peace."

"Peace?" Pierre says. "She's clearly in pain."

"No, she's dead here," he says. "You can't feel any pain if you're dead."

"Why would you take these pictures in the first place?" Pierre asks. "It's perverse. Taking pictures of a dead person and showing them around. You did the same thing when Dad died. I don't want to see pictures of my dead parents."

"There's nothing ugly about death—maybe it's about time you realized that."

"Would you please just respect that I don't want to? I don't want to see, and that's that," Pierre says. "A grieving son does not want to look at pictures of his parents in the moment they died."

"Grieving . . ." Nils mutters. He takes a sip of beer.

"What?" Pierre says. "What do you mean?"

"You sure do seem to be in deep sorrow."

"Shut up, we all grieve differently!"

Silence around the table.

"Can't you just accept it?" Pierre says. "I don't want to see pictures of Mom dead. Put that shit away."

Nils doesn't respond. He picks up the phone and looks through it, smiling and nervous, browsing aimlessly among the various apps, and slowly the feeling of being wronged begins to emanate from him. Pierre doesn't notice at all, but Benjamin can certainly feel it as Nils's umbrage at being admonished and humiliated unfurls into a state of pique he battles in silence. He gets up and goes inside.

"Pierre," Benjamin whispers. "That was unnecessary, don't you think?"

"But he's nuts, right? I wanted to chew him out even back at the hospital when he started taking photos of her. But when he forces me to look at them, it drives me crazy."

"We have to try to get through this so we can carry out Mom's final wishes. So we need to not fight."

Pierre doesn't respond. He tilts the little bowl of chips Nils has put out, but there are none left. He looks down at the table for a moment, then gets up and walks inside. Benjamin can see his back through the open kitchen window, can hear his firm voice.

"I'm sorry, I didn't mean to be so hard on you about the pictures."

Nils, sitting at the kitchen table, looks up.

"No worries," he says. "It was the wrong time to show them to you."

Pierre puts out his arms, Nils stands up, and it sounds like applause as they clap each other on the back. Benjamin feels the skin of his face pulling and realizes he's smiling. The hug is brief, but it doesn't matter because it definitely happened, and for a moment or two Benjamin sits on the patio with a sense of absolute satisfaction, like when you're unspooling a tangled net after a night of strong winds and bountiful hauls, and it seems hopeless, like you might have to throw the whole net away. But then you turn one loop in an unexpected direction and you hardly have to use any force and there's a rustle and the net releases itself, flowing out of your hands and arranging itself neatly on the hooks on the wall.

Pierre and Nils appear on the stone steps. Pierre holds up three cans of beer.

"Bro time in the sauna!"

And they walk down the narrow path to the lake. They stand in front of each other on the little sauna porch and take off their clothes; slowly and rather reluctantly, the brothers are uncovered. Benjamin sees the identical burn scars on his brothers' shins, from the time they rubbed erasers on each other's skin until they shrieked and it smelled like burnt hair and flesh and Dad noticed what they were up to and slapped the erasers out of their hands. He sees Pierre's foot fungus, the red skin between his toes. Benjamin observes Nils's bare back in the sauna. The collection of moles is still there, like a scattershot of brown dots that landed between his shoulder blades.

10

THE GHOST HAND

Red-fingered and howling, Pierre and Benjamin had been smacking each other's hands with a flyswatter, but soon they were shushed and banned from the kitchen by Mom and Dad. There needed to be peace and quiet, because important things were happening around the kitchen table. Benjamin and Pierre sat on the stairs with a good view of the well-thumbed papers, the stubs and formulas on the table. Dad picked up one piece of paper, stared sternly at it, and put it back where it had been. Nils was at the short end of the table, signing a document; Mom swiftly placed it aside and provided another one. Mom and Dad had been doing this for a long time, sitting with Nils and making strategies, muttering in grave tones, pointing and exchanging papers. Today was the deadline for applying to high schools, and this was it. All the papers had to be sent in so their eldest son could be guided forth into the academic world.

For a number of years, Nils's efforts at school had given him special standing with Mom and Dad. He was the family's great hope, the one that would do something with his life. It had always been that way. His performance in first grade was so outstanding that he had skipped second and gone straight to third, and each time he came home from school he had something in his backpack to show off, one triumph or another. Writing assignments that their parents eagerly read aloud to each other, or schoolwork that was examined and discussed. When Nils came home with the results of an important exam, Mom always gathered the family, wouldn't open the brown envelope until everyone was present, and she took out her reading glasses and decoded the test results in concentrated silence while Nils stood next to her, waiting with nervous posture, one hand on his waist and the other resting on his thigh. At last, when Mom understood the breadth of Nils's success, she shook her head and peered over her glasses at him with a smile. "You're ridiculous," she said. And always the same thing as she held the test up to Benjamin and Pierre: "This is how it's done!"

It was raining out. No lights were on, aside from the ceiling fixture, which cast a yellow glow over Nils's future on the table. Benjamin and Pierre sat in the murky dark of the stairs, watching what went on in the kitchen, listening to these pivotal conversations.

"Are you sure you want to choose German?" Mom asked, looking down at a document.

"Yes, I think so," Nils replied.

"Well," said Mom. "It's just too bad about French. I think you would have loved that language—it's so refined and beautiful."

"I was going to see if you can add a language outside of the curriculum, so I can study both French and German. Just want to get used to the school and my work first."

The proud parents exchanged glances. Benjamin looked at Pierre and saw that he was slowly extending his middle finger in Nils's direction. Benjamin snickered and followed suit.

"Fuck you," whispered Pierre.

"Fuck you," whispered Benjamin.

"Fuck you forever," whispered Pierre. Benjamin shoved Pierre in the side.

"Oh no," Benjamin said, looking at his middle finger.

"What?" Pierre asked.

"Can't you see? Ghost hand."

Pierre watched as Benjamin's hand changed, his fingers spreading until they looked like gnarled branches on a dead tree, and the hand suddenly turned toward him. Pierre leapt up and dashed down the stairs and Benjamin ran after him, chasing his brother through the kitchen, then capturing him and shoving him to the floor.

"Ghost hand!" he cried. "It's not me! It's someone else controlling my hand!"

Benjamin flipped Pierre onto his back and used his knees to pin his arms to the floor, and then he tickled Pierre's belly and chest and armpits.

"Stop!" Pierre shouted, trying to get away.

"How can I stop? It's not me!"

Benjamin tickled him harder; Pierre couldn't breathe, his face twisted in a happy grin, and even though Benjamin could hear the protests from the kitchen table, Nils's roars and Dad's horrified noises, he kept at it, because there was light and air in Pierre's bubbly laughter, and Pierre laughed without making a sound and twisted his head right and left and right again, and then he started to cry. Benjamin let go.

"What's wrong?" he asked. "Did it hurt?"

Pierre didn't answer. He turned onto his side and buried his face in his hands. Benjamin stood up and saw a puddle of urine gleaming on the wooden floor, and he saw the dark stain over the fly of Pierre's jeans. Molly reached the puddle first; she gave it a cursory glance and walked away.

"Mom . . . ," Benjamin said, nodding at the puddle.

"Oh my God," she said, standing up.

She found a dish sponge and dropped it into the liquid, then took the sponge to the sink and wrung it out. The pee ran down her fingers when she squeezed it, but she wasn't bothered. She was unfazed by bodily fluids and always had been. Certainly she was upset whenever Dad forgot to put up the toilet seat and left dribbles on it; she would shout at him, but she never bothered to wipe it up, just sat down and let the backs of her thighs absorb the pee. Mom made another pass with the dishrag. Benjamin went to Pierre, who was crying on the floor.

"It's no big deal," Benjamin said. He put a hand on his brother's back. "It happens to me all the time."

"No it doesn't," Pierre said between sobs.

"Sure it does," he said. "Hold on!"

Benjamin pretended to check himself; he stared up at the ceiling.

Pierre looked up from behind his fingers. "Now I peed *my* pants," Benjamin said.

Pierre laughed through his tears. Mom wrung out the last bit in the sink. "Go change your clothes," she told Pierre. Mom took her newspaper and cigarettes and went to the living room. Dad concluded the ceremony at the kitchen table and stuffed the thick bundle of papers into an envelope. He let his slack, bestial tongue hang from his mouth as he drew the row of stamps across it; then he stuck them on the envelope. An enormous number of stamps. He handed the letter to Nils.

"This is a big day," said Dad. His voice broke. "My big boy," he said. Sobbing, he hugged his son. Nils's clumsy attempts to participate in the hug. His temple against Dad's, his arms limp, like tubes of flesh around Dad's waist.

"Time to go," Dad said, and Nils ran upstairs to get changed.

Benjamin went out to sit on the stone steps, gazing up the slope and the narrow path where Nils would soon vanish. The tractor path was the only way in. And it was the only way out. It was like a skinny gravel intestine that linked the cottage with reality. And if it were to become overgrown, this place would go insane; it would have lost all reason. Sometimes Benjamin just sat and stared at the path, mostly to reassure himself that it was still there, where he had last seen it. A few times each summer, Dad would go out with the scythe and cut back the grass that always grew between the tire tracks, to ensure free passage. The children always followed along but had to stay behind him; when they got too close he gave a shrill cry and pointed at the blade of the scythe. "This can chop off your leg without you even feeling it." While his brothers got bored and trooped off, Benjamin would follow his dad all the way up, standing behind him and supervising. When they were done, they had a look at what they'd accomplished. "That's how it should look," said

Dad. "Like a long grass pussy." He laughed and tousled Benjamin's hair, and they walked back down the path.

Benjamin turned his eyes to Nils's moped, which was parked outside the root cellar. Nils wasn't even fourteen, but Mom and Dad trusted him; they knew he was a cautious driver. Benjamin had never been allowed to try out the moped, but when Nils first got it he had let him stand next to the machine, rev it in neutral, and Benjamin felt its power and it dawned on him just what the moped was capable of. It was a way out, to the other side. Now Nils had brand-new opportunities to escape. The kid who was always making himself scarce suddenly had the means to disappear faster than ever, and go even farther away. And Benjamin stood next to the moped and revved with his right hand while Nils carefully watched over his vehicle. Benjamin realized the moped would change everything, that it would leave him conclusively on his own, and he revved and revved, making the engine roar to drown out his own despair.

Every morning, Nils took off for the town, where he'd gotten a summer job in a grocery store, but he also came back each evening with tastes of the city. At the end of his shift, Nils cleaned the bulk candy aisle and instead of throwing out what customers had dropped on the floor, he gathered it in a bag and gave it to Benjamin and Pierre. They poured the contents out on the kitchen table, picked hairs and dust bunnies out of the pile, rubbed away dirt and grime, culled the pieces that had taken the most punishment, the trampled gummy bananas that still sported shoe prints, the sweet rum sprinkles that had been flattened like five-kronor coins. And then they ran down to the beach with their spoils so they could eat them in peace. It became a tradition: Nils came home with dirty candy and Benjamin and Pierre sat down by the lake, gazing out at the water, stuffing their mouths, and sometimes the candy squeaked and crunched in their teeth when they got a piece of grit and they sputtered and spat it out on the rocks and giggled.

Pierre got changed and sat down on the stone steps with Benjamin to watch as Nils took off. Nils was getting ready for his journey. He put on the overlarge helmet and pressed on the saddle to see if the tires had enough air. He placed the envelope in a plastic bag and fastened it to the cargo rack and Dad checked to make sure he'd done a good job. Then he headed out into the world, first to a mailbox to secure his future, then to work, and Benjamin watched him vanish up the slope, listening to the sound of the engine, which was eventually drowned out by the wind, and he knew the feelings in Nils's body, because he was on his way now, on his way to the other end of the gravel path, and he had been there himself, those times he was allowed to accompany his parents when they went grocery shopping. It was like a gravitational pull, the string of gravel like a gateway to another dimension, you went fast and sort of lost control until at last you were spat out on the other end, onto asphalt, well-maintained, to a place that looked like a community, where there were houses on either side of the road. Sometimes, in his solitude, he thought about the other end of the gravel path, and how life began there.

Dad sat down next to Benjamin and Pierre.

"Well then, boys," he said, looking out at the yard. "What damn shitty weather we're having."

Molly snuck up the stairs and crept into Benjamin's lap. Dad quickly grabbed her, trapped her by pressing her to his body, and gently stroked her head. Dad had decided to tame her fear, force her to accept his love. A few times each day he chased her down to show tenderness.

"Why don't you cuddle her a little too," he said to Pierre. Pierre ran his hand over her head, and Benjamin saw the fear streaming off her; she was stiff and afraid and on alert, ready to run as soon as she got the chance.

"What are we going to do today, with such shitty weather?" Dad said.

"I don't know," Benjamin replied.

"Why don't you go have an adventure in the forest?"

Pierre and Benjamin didn't respond.

"You can take Molly," said Dad.

"She never wants to come anywhere with us," said Pierre.

"Sure she does. Benjamin can take care of her."

When Dad relinquished his hold on Molly, she immediately tried to escape. Dad cursed, watched the dog vanish into the house, heard her whine, and from the murky dark inside, through the veils of cigarette smoke in the living room, they heard Mom's voice, contorted and childish, as she called for her: "Hey there, hi there." And Molly slipped into the fog.

Pierre and Benjamin put on their raincoats and boots and went out. They followed the power line that ran from the house and up through the fir trees, and Benjamin thought that as long as that black thread in the air was within sight he would know his way back. There was a gentle rain; the forest seemed heavy. They leapt between the slippery stones. They went farther in than usual, behind the overgrown path that led to the dam, past the big boulders that lay scattered in the enormous swamp. They kept walking in where the forest grew more dense.

"Look at that," Pierre said, pointing up at a little rise.

Past the tall trees was an electrical substation. A small building surrounded by rows of poles, black spears with white tips, like firework rockets aimed at the sky. And outside of them were two larger structures, towering poles like steel spiderwebs on either side of the building, sending out their black lines in three directions through the forest.

"What is that?" Pierre said.

"That's where all the electricity comes from," Benjamin told him. He took a few steps toward the building. "Let's go take a look."

A tall security fence surrounded the building; on it were yellow signs showing red lightning bolts. Benjamin looked up and saw the power lines, black wires dividing the low, gray sky into perfect fields. He looked at the building, its mottled façade; the bricks were coming loose and lay in little piles at its base. Two small windows on the back side made it look like a house. When they got to the front, they saw that the door was wide open.

"Did it blow open?"

"Doesn't look like it," said Benjamin. "It's been broken into."

"Why would someone break in here?"

"I don't know."

Benjamin and Pierre stood side by side at the fence, their fingers through the gaps, trying to peer in through the open door, but they couldn't see a thing, could only hear the sound of electricity from inside, a dull rumbling that didn't sound like anything Benjamin had ever heard before, almost mystical, as if he could make out only part of the sound, as if there were frequencies he couldn't hear. And he thought maybe that was true, that electricity is actually much louder, like a restless, prolonged screech, and the noise is unbearable for the creatures of the forest, but his human ears could perceive only a low hum, as if the electricity wanted to broadcast a reminder of its existence, and a warning: Don't come any closer.

They walked on, into the forest. They picked blueberries and mashed them into their faces, pretending it was blood and that they were badly wounded. They threw rocks at a dead tree trunk, and each time they hit their mark there was a strange, hollow echo through the forest. They used a stick to poke at an anthill and watched the whole mound start to teem with life. They waded through a marsh so deep that it almost came over their boots, the water pressing the rubber to their shins. They found scat and did what their dad always did: poked at it with a stick and raised their eyes, grim, to see where the animal had gone. They walked farther and farther into the forest, and when Benjamin looked up to orient himself again, the electrical wires were gone. He couldn't see them anywhere. He turned around and turned around again. Identical scenery in every direction. The exact same hilly woods, the same heavy pines, under the same rainy sky. All of a sudden, he panicked.

"Come on!" he shouted to Pierre. "We have to go back."

He took off running, Pierre close on his heels. He heard his own breathing, branches cracking under his feet, looking for clues in the land. He stopped, turned around, slowly becoming certain: he had run in the wrong direction. And he turned around to run just as fast in a different direction, Pierre following. His foot landed in a marshy spot, his boot filled with water and his leg became heavy, his steps squishy, but he kept running, his eyes searching for the electrical lines that would lead them home. He stopped, out of breath, hands on his knees. Pierre caught up and Benjamin could see that he was flushed, that red spots were blooming on his neck as they always did when he was scared.

"Don't we know where we are?" Pierre asked.

"Sure we do," Benjamin said.

"Then how do we get home?"

BENJAMIN CALLED UP a memory of hiking with his father in the woods; his father had said that if he ever got lost he should walk toward the sun. "That way you'll always make it back to the lake eventually." He looked up, tried to find a spot, a bright point in the gray sky, but everything was milky and shapeless.

They walked slowly. Benjamin felt that the forest was getting bigger and taller, or that they were getting smaller, as if they were slowly sinking into it and if the bog rose another two inches they would drown. They sat down on a large rock. It was getting darker and lighter—dusk was falling even as the layer of clouds scattered and the tops of the trees captured the last of the sunshine. Pierre began to cry, and Benjamin got mad at him.

"What are you crying for?"

"We're never going to get home."

"Stop it!" he hissed. "Just stop it."

Benjamin imagined that eventually Mom and Dad would wonder where the kids had got to, and they'd come looking in the forest. But time passed and the light grew dim. They'd been sitting there for a long time, it felt like two hours, maybe three, when Benjamin suddenly heard something far off in the forest. A bright rumbling sound he recognized immediately, a sound that he otherwise associated with despair and loneliness but that now sparked hope—it was Nils's moped. He realized that his older brother was on his way home from work, that he was whizzing down the gravel road above the cottage.

"Run!" Benjamin cried to Pierre.

And they ran toward the sound of the engine, heard Nils revving hard, heard the engine scream as he downshifted on an uphill stretch, and they ran over the rises and hills, through the thickets and between the trees, and suddenly everything fell into place around Benjamin. He saw the puddles in the excavator tracks they'd balanced across earlier, he saw the piles of timber and the leaning firs, and then the worn electrical poles with black strips of electricity above them that ran through the forest. They hurried down the tractor path and could see the cottage between the trees. Nils's moped was standing hot next to the patio. Benjamin could see Mom and Dad sitting outside the sauna down by the lake. Lit candles and bottles on the table. Nils was unpacking a bag from the store in the living room. He'd bought cola, still cold and pearled with sweat, and cheese curls, which he poured into a bowl. He tossed a bag to Benjamin when he spotted him.

"Damaged candy," Benjamin called to Pierre. Pierre came into the living room.

"Shouldn't we go tell Mom and Dad what happened?" Pierre asked.

"No, why would we?"

"Because we were lost. For a really long time."

"But now we're back," Benjamin replied. "Want some candy?"

Nils took a few steps toward the window and looked down at the lake, reassuring himself that Mom and Dad were still down there, and then he went over to the TV. Without a moment of hesitation, he plugged it in and turned it on. Benjamin watched mutely as Nils pulled up an easy chair so he could hear the low volume, and he sat down with the cheese curls in his lap. Nils did the most unimaginable things with a sense of confidence that Benjamin simply couldn't comprehend. Pierre and Benjamin sat down on the rug behind Nils and poured out the candy between them.

"How did it go with the envelope?" Benjamin asked. "Did you mail it?"

"Yeah," Nils said.

"Great," said Benjamin.

Benjamin was chewing on a red race car that got stuck first between his teeth and then on the roof of his mouth; his tongue hurt when he shoved it away.

"Super important that you sent off that envelope," Benjamin said.

Nils looked at Benjamin, then turned back to the TV.

"Now the whole family can relax," Benjamin said.

"Right," Nils replied. "Because it's not exactly likely that you two will ever get into a single school, you idiots."

Benjamin and Pierre looked at the back of Nils's head, taking in his hunched posture as he leaned toward the TV. Benjamin stood up without a sound. He knew Nils's weak points, and which one was weakest. Nils's hair was sparse on the crown of his head; there was a patch the size of a snuffbox where you could see the pale skin of his scalp through the thin strands. Mom liked to put sunscreen on it so he wouldn't get a sunburn, but she usually used too much, which meant Nils was often walking around with a sticky patch on the top of his head. Benjamin and Pierre sometimes teased him about his bald spot, but only when they were sure Mom couldn't hear. Benjamin snuck up and cautiously gathered up the sparse hair on the top of Nils's head by swirling his finger around the affected area. Nils gave a start and turned around.

"Fucking stop it!" he shouted.

"You're such a good student, *sweetheart,*" said Benjamin.

Snickering, Benjamin sat back down. Pierre and Benjamin waited a moment, and then Pierre stood, snuck over, and did the same thing. Nils flailed his fist wildly behind him, but missed. He got up and stood there holding his bowl of cheese curls. And then Nils's eyes crossed slightly, as they always did in the evening when he was tired, and his brothers pounced on the fact immediately and mocked him by crossing their own eyes.

"I swear, I'm going to kill you both," Nils said, sitting back down.

Benjamin, who could see their parents' fights coming long before they themselves were able to, was blind to what was about to happen to him. He snuck up once more, his finger raised, as Pierre tried to muffle his giggles by covering his mouth. No sooner had his finger landed on Nils's head than Nils whipped around and lashed out again, with a hard blow that hit Benjamin in the shoulder. Nils had turned so violently that the bowl of cheese curls had fallen from his lap, and they scattered across the floor.

"Dammit!" Nils shouted, looking at the ruins.

Benjamin realized that they were out of chances to control the situation. He took a few steps toward the kitchen, but Nils quickly caught up and captured him in his arms. Nils was bigger and stronger, and he shoved Benjamin to the floor. He pinned both of Benjamin's hands down with his own left hand and punched him in the temple with his right. Benjamin's ears rang and for a moment he lost consciousness; it returned just as Nils dealt another blow and another and another, his fist hammering into Benjamin's head. He couldn't see anything anymore, just heard the dull thuds against his skull, and Pierre's desperate voice in the background: "Stop! Stop hitting him!"

The blows ceased. He felt Nils relax his grip. He lay there, saw Nils looking out the window and dashing up the stairs. After a few seconds the front door opened, and Mom and Dad came inside with bottles, plates, and glasses. Benjamin tried to get up, because he didn't want them to see him lying there, didn't want them to find out what had happened.

"Nils punched Benjamin in the head," Pierre cried.

Mom stood in the doorway and looked at Benjamin. "What did you two do to Nils this time?" she said.

"Nils was watching TV," said Benjamin.

"What the hell are you talking about?" Mom said. "What kind of brother tattles on his sibling?"

Benjamin gingerly touched his face, to find out if he was bleeding.

"What did you do to him? What cruel things did you say to him this time?" Mom asked. When they didn't answer, she took a step into the room and screamed, "Answer me! Tell me what you did to Nils!"

She turned to Pierre.

"What happened?" she asked.

"We were playing in the woods and we got lost."

"No we didn't," Benjamin said.

"Did too, we were lost for hours, and I cried."

Mom looked at her sons, that half-open mouth, her shock and hatred. "Nasty brats," she said, then turned and walked into the hall. Benjamin heard her heavy tread on the stairs. He was still sitting on the floor, listening as she opened the door to Nils's room, closed it, and then the muffled murmur of Nils's lies. He tentatively got to his feet. Pierre sat down with the pile of candy on the living room floor. He set aside a ten-öre coin that had tagged along in the bag, selected a raspberry gummy that seemed unharmed, and popped it into his mouth. Benjamin tackled him and wrestled him to the floor.

"No, not the ghost hand," Pierre shrieked. Benjamin used his knees to pin Pierre's hands and tickled his chest, belly, and armpits. Pierre laughed, tried to get away, tried to yell at him to stop, but his red grimace couldn't produce words. After a few seconds, an anxious expression passed over his face. "Stop for real, Benjamin. I'm going to pee my pants." Benjamin pressed his knees down more firmly, tickled him harder, and Pierre stopped laughing. He tried to wriggle away, he yanked and lurched with his whole body, but Benjamin was heavy on top of him. He got one hand free and smacked Benjamin in the chest and face. His desperate look, as he hit and hit without success, and then came the tears as the puddle of pee formed beneath him.

11

2 : O O   P . M .

He rounds the last curve and soon the red wooden house emerges from among the trees. He sees the overgrown lot, glances up over the impressive firs, which make the place seem so small. The tall grass rustles under the car. He drives all the way up to the root cellar and turns off the engine. The brothers sit in the car for a moment and look out.

They're back.

They open the doors, squeeze themselves out of the cool, temperature-controlled interior, and step straight out into summer. The sounds of the cottage reach them, the familiar swish of the swallows coming and going, patient bumblebees and anxious wasps. Insects everywhere, one in each flower. And all across the yard, the wind makes its presence known, catching the treetops, whistling through the firs, and fanning the car, which pops and creaks after its long journey.

"Should we go in the house first?" Pierre says. "And make sure everything's okay?"

"No," Benjamin says. "I want to do it now."

Neither Nils nor Pierre responds, but they set their suitcases down and take a few steps toward Benjamin, and side by side the three of them walk down the little path between the house and the barn and slip into the forest.

This is Benjamin's forest.

He has it inside him, has carried it with him all these years. He knows every rock, every tricky trail, every fallen birch. It's all closer than he remembers—the marsh, which was once eerie, endless, now takes seven steps to cross. The giant, mysterious boulders are now perfectly ordinary. But the spruces are still inconceivable. When he looks up at the treetops he feels dizzy, as if he's going to fall headlong through them.

"Are we going the right way?" Pierre asks.

"Yes," Benjamin replies. "Just keep walking straight ahead. Past that rise there."

Benjamin is bringing up the rear and studies the backs of his brothers' necks as they look down to see where to place their feet. They're walking more slowly now, like you do when you're approaching a large animal, cautious steps through the dry forest. He'd hoped that it would all be gone, that the fence would have been removed, the building leveled, that there would be bushes and thickets where its foundation once stood. But it's not so, of course. The substation is still there among the pines, and the fence is there, and the poles. It's as if it has always been there, and always will be. The brothers stand at a distance.

"We don't need to get any closer," Pierre says.

"Yes, we do," Benjamin says.

Benjamin walks ahead and his brothers follow. The windows are broken. Weeds are growing between the bricks of the façade. The black cables that used to extend from the tall poles, supplying the world, have been removed.

"It's no longer in use," Benjamin says.

"No, doesn't seem like it," says Nils. "The station is so old. I'm sure it couldn't handle modern-day standards."

Benjamin looks up at the building.

"Do you remember the sound?" he asks.

His brothers don't respond, just gaze at the façade. "That sad hum of the electricity. Don't you remember?"

"Yes," Nils murmurs.

Benjamin looks at his brothers, who are reluctantly moving toward the tall fence. He peers into the black opening. The door is wide open. Its busted lock still hangs down like a broken limb.

"To think that someone broke in," Benjamin said. "I don't get it. There couldn't have been anything of value in there, right?"

"Copper," says Nils. "Hardly anything is as conductive as copper. And copper is worth a lot of money."

Benjamin's eyes follow the fence, see how it surrounds the little building, and over there is the iron gate, the way in, and he sees the shape of himself as a child, the little boy pulling loose from his brothers and walking to the opening. He lays his forehead against the metal mesh. He hears his brothers' heavy breathing. They're standing side by side.

"What happened?" Benjamin says.

Nils and Pierre look down at their hands, which have pushed through the holes. He can tell from their posture that they don't want to be here. But they have no choice.

"All my life, I've blamed myself," Benjamin says. "But I also had two brothers with me."

"We were children," says Pierre.

"Yeah," says Benjamin. "And we were brothers. Remember what Dad always said? He said we should be happy that we're brothers, because brothers are the strongest bond there is."

Benjamin does not turn to look at Pierre and Nils, just stares stubbornly into the dark doorway.

From the corner of his eye he sees Pierre pat his pockets, take out a cigarette, which he lights in the shelter of his cupped hand.

"I think about that day all the time," says Nils.

The sun is lower in the sky now, the shadows of the pines leaving black stains on the brilliant green blueberry bushes around the building.

"When I got back to the house that afternoon . . ." Nils laughs suddenly. "I lay down in the hammock and listened to music. I thought, if I do everything I usually do, it will be like nothing ever happened. I knew you were dead, because I saw it happen. I stood right here and I saw it all. And I thought I would feel regret or fear. And maybe I did. But you know what the strongest feeling was?"

Benjamin doesn't answer, just watches Nils in silence.

"Relief," says Nils.

"Jesus Christ," says Pierre. "Stop it." He spots a rock and kicks it.

"If we're going to talk about it, we should talk about it,

right?" Nils says and turns back to Benjamin again. "I'm sorry for what I did. I was in shock, but that's no excuse. And I hate myself for it. But have you forgotten what it was like? Have you forgotten how you and Pierre tortured me? I still have all my diaries. I read them sometimes. Every day, I wished you were dead. And then it finally happened."

Benjamin observes Nils. His slightly crossed eyes. He sees the scar between his temple and his eye from the time he fell on the edge of a pool as a child. His smooth, childlike skin, and the dark brown eyes that have such a lovely glow when the sun strikes them. Benjamin feels a sudden longing for his brother. He wants to feel Nils close, he wants Nils to hold him tight to keep him from falling toward the treetops and tumbling into the sky. He places a hand on his big brother's shoulder, feels how thin he is, the knobs of his bones through his shirt. It feels strange and unfamiliar, but he leaves his hand there and Nils places a hand over Benjamin's, pats it awkwardly. They look at each other and nod. His gentle smile.

They walk in a line back through the forest, heavy steps through the glades where they ran as children. They take it slow on the last little steep bit down the hill, catch themselves among the trees so as not to lose control, and tumble out into the blazing sun.

12

THE ARC OF LIGHT

It was Midsummer Eve.

He remembered the stout ladies who sold coffee and buns behind the spindly-legged tables. He remembered the old man with the clattery tombola who pretended to slam the hatch closed each time a child's finger got too close, and the kids hooting and scattering and edging back again. A lotto board, five kronor per ticket, he remembered winning first prize, a chocolate bar, and he felt the melted chocolate swimming around in there beneath the paper. He remembered the coffee-stained picnic blankets where families sat uncomfortably, opening their thermoses. He remembered that the Midsummer pole was decorated by women but erected by men. Great cheer when it was finally upright, scattered applause that faded in the breeze. It was windier than usual, the speaker system swayed, the accordion music sounded distant and eerie. He remembered that Molly got nervous when the wind snagged the treetops and rustled their crowns above the meadow. He remembered that they had sat off to the side, separate from the rest of the crowd. As always, when the family was somewhere where there were other people, they participated without truly being part of the group. The brothers were grubby but dressed up. Mom had tried to tame Pierre's hair with spit. Dad slowly peeled off a few bills for the boys, who ran off to buy soda. None of them really wanted to dance around the pole, Mom stood waving from the circle, and they danced to the little frogs song, but soon they snuck off one after the next, back to the blanket, and Mom was left alone, Molly in her arms, swaying back and forth to the song about musicians, and after a while she came back, exhausted but full of energy, giving a falsetto cry as she sat down.

"Well, what do you say, shall we get going?" Dad leapt to his feet.

"Yes, let's go!"

The family had a Midsummer tradition: each year, they drove to the E-road and stopped at a roadside pub for lunch. This was the only time all summer they ate at a restaurant. It was always the same pub, always empty on Midsummer Eve, when everyone else was at home eating herring luncheons with their families. Dad and Mom sat down at their favorite table, the one by the window with a view of the highway.

"Have you got a charcuterie board?" Dad asked the server.

"No, I'm sorry."

"Have you got anything with salami?"

"Salami? Yes, there's salami on some of the pizzas."

"Can I get that salami on a little plate?"

The server stared at Dad, confused. "Okay . . . ," he said. "I guess that's fine."

"Great, there's our charcuterie board. Do you have ice-cold vodka?"

"Of course," the server replied.

After a while he returned carrying tumblers with vodka in the bottom, which Mom and Dad sipped. Dad made a face.

"Room temperature," he said, waving at the server. "Can we get a bowl of ice?"

"Wasn't it cold enough?" the server asked.

"Sure. We just want it a little colder."

Mom and Dad exchanged smiles as he disappeared, experienced drinkers willing to overlook the clumsy attempts of amateurs. The ice cubes creaked as they dropped them in, and they raised their glasses and drank.

It was a lunch that slowly fell silent. The conversations got slower, Dad and Mom ate lazily, ordered more drinks. Dad anxiously tried to make eye contact with the server. They were no longer speaking, aside from a quick "Hey" as they had yet another vodka. Dad usually got listless when he drank, distant but harmless, but this time was different. Benjamin noticed that he was getting unusually testy. He sternly called out "Hello" when the server didn't notice he was waving. Benjamin used his straw to blow bubbles in his soda, and Dad told him to stop. After a while Benjamin did it again, and Dad took the straw away and tried to tear it in half. But it didn't work, the plastic was tough, indestructible, and Dad tried again, baring his teeth with the effort. When he found that the straw was still intact, he threw it on the floor. Mom looked up from Molly, who was in her lap, took note of the turbulence, and turned back again. Benjamin didn't move, afraid to look at his father. He didn't understand. He realized that something was out of the ordinary. From now on, he would be on his guard.

Afterward, they got in the car. Benjamin was always extra watchful in here, because it seemed like the worst of their drama happened in the car, when the family was enclosed in such a small space. This was where Mom and Dad had their wildest fights, when Dad swerved as he tried to tune the radio or when Mom missed a turn and Dad yelled in rage and twisted his neck to watch the exit vanishing behind them.

"Take it easy," Mom muttered as Dad turned out of the parking lot.

"Yeah, yeah," Dad said.

Benjamin was in the middle of the back seat, that was his spot, because from there he could keep an eye on his parents, on the road, and on his brothers to either side. He was the family's silent command hub, controlling events from the center. As Dad went to turn onto the county road, he spun the wheel too far and the car brushed into a grove of saplings just off the shoulder, branches and twigs scraping hard across the windshield.

"Hey!" Mom cried.

"Yeah, yeah," Dad said.

He drove off, revving the engine hard and long at low gear, and when he finally shifted up, the car lurched, the boys' heads bobbing left to right in back. Benjamin concentrated on watching Dad's eyes in the rearview mirror, saw him blink as the car veered back and forth. Benjamin didn't dare say anything; all he could do was sit quietly and concentrate as if he were the one driving. Through the side window he could see the car approaching the ditch. Pierre was nonchalantly reading a comic book he'd found on the floor. But Nils was pressing his head to the window, carefully following along as the car veered dangerously from one side of the road to the other. The county road narrowed and turned to gravel and the trees towered on either side of the car. Dad sped through the forest, and they were close now; as they climbed the steep hill just before they would turn onto the tractor path and descend toward the cottage, Benjamin thought they might make it after all.

As they rounded the final curve, Dad lost control in the porous gravel. The car let go and careened freely across the surface, its wheels locked. Dad tried to counter the skid and the car ended up in the ditch on the other side of the road. Benjamin was thrown forward and came to rest over the gearshift; his brothers landed in the footwells. Dad looked around in confusion. Mom had hugged Molly tight to her chest as they left the road, and she quickly checked to make sure she wasn't injured. Then she turned around.

"Is everyone okay?"

The brothers unfurled themselves again and got back in their seats. The car was at an angle, the three brothers pressed to the right. Dad started the engine.

"What are you doing?" Mom asked.

"We have to get out," Dad said.

"There's no way—we'll have to call someone," said Mom.

"Nonsense."

He tried to drive back onto the road, hitting the gas until the engine screamed, dirt and rocks striking the undercarriage, but the car stood still.

"Shit!" Dad shouted, hitting the gas again. Pierre opened his door.

"Close the door!" Dad cried. "For Christ's sake, close the door!"

Benjamin reached over Pierre and pulled the door shut as the engine howled ferociously, and Mom shouted to be heard over it: "It's not going to work!"

Dad put it in reverse and revved the engine and this time the car got traction and worked its way out of the ditch. Dad stopped in the center of the gravel road to put it in first. Pierre opened his door again.

"I want to walk home from here," he said.

"Me too," said Benjamin.

Benjamin saw his father's sneer in the mirror.

"For Christ's sake, what did I just say about the door!"

He turned halfway around and slapped indiscriminately at the boys. Molly tore herself from Mom's grip and tried to find a way out of the car.

"Don't open the door while the engine is on!"

The brothers tried to shield their heads as his fist flew through the air. Dad got Benjamin in the shoulders a few times, and Pierre got a whack on the thigh. But Nils came off worst, because he was right in the way of Dad's oscillating swings and couldn't dodge the fist flying back and forth, so his face took blow after blow. "Stop!" Mom shouted, trying to grab Dad's arm, but he was somewhere else, no one could reach him. Pierre's first instinct was to flee, he fumbled with the door, trying to get out, while Benjamin had the opposite instinct. He huddled against Pierre's side and pulled the door shut, closing himself and his brothers in with the blows.

"It's closed, Dad!" he screamed. "It's closed!"

Another swing of the fist, and a grunt, and everything went quiet. The blows stopped and Benjamin dared to peer out between his fingers. Dad was calm, looking at the steering wheel. Then he put the car in first gear and drove, and now all the brothers sat up and looked at the road, watching Dad's slack hands on the wheel, following every movement as he guided the car down the tractor path and parked it outside the house. None of the brothers dared to open the door.

"I'm going to lie down," Dad said as he stepped out of the car. Benjamin watched him through the window, between the front seats: Dad steadied himself against the tree trunks that lined the driveway, took broad, unsteady steps up the stone stairs, and he was gone. Mom got out of the car, opened the door on Nils's side, and signaled to the brothers to climb out. They gathered outside the car. Benjamin looked at his mother, her swimmy eyes, the crooked smile she always wore when she'd had too much to drink and was trying to make sense of things in a world that was suddenly incomprehensible.

"Are you all okay?"

She gently stroked Nils's face.

"Sweetie," she said, inspecting a cut on his chin. "I'll talk to Dad about this and he will apologize to you. But I think he needs to get some sleep first. Do you understand?"

The boys nodded. Mom put her hand on the hood of the car to steady herself, turned a gentle smile on Pierre, and patted his cheek. She looked at him for a long time but still didn't notice that his eyes were welling with tears, didn't see how he was trembling.

"Dad and I are going to nap for a while," she said. "And then we'll have a proper family meeting about this."

She handed Molly to Benjamin.

"Can you take care of her for a while?"

And she slowly walked off down the path. She stopped short, as if she'd just thought of something, but then she kept going, past the root cellar and up the stone steps to the house. Only once she was gone did Pierre let himself burst into tears, and Benjamin and Nils held him from either side, and Nils grabbed Benjamin, and as the three of them hugged each other next to the car Benjamin felt, for the first time in a long time, that the brothers were together.

That was when Molly disappeared. She wasn't herself after the car ride, she was whining uneasily, first pacing back and forth nervously along the path, and then she suddenly dashed into the trees as if she had made up her mind to run away. Benjamin called after her, first encouragingly, *"Hey there, hi there,"* then sternly, "Come here right now!" All three brothers called for her, but she paid no attention and kept going up the hill; she no longer wanted to be a part of it.

And that's how the brothers ended up walking into the forest that afternoon, to follow the frightened dog, and at last they caught her. Benjamin picked her up, saw the fear in her eyes, felt her heart beating through her rib cage.

They kept going. He remembered that Pierre was wearing a white shirt that Mom had carefully tucked into his jeans but was now hanging over his waistband. He remembered that they walked over roots that looked like ancient fingers. He remembered that they heard the cuckoo somewhere in the pines, and that they imitated its call. He remembered that they scraped pieces of bark from one tree and floated them in the stream that flowed down the forested slope to the lake. And they kept walking up the hill, and it wasn't something any of them really wished to do, they didn't even say it out loud, but they ended up there anyway, on the narrow path that led to the electrical substation. They could hear the sound of electricity from far off, like an organ in the distance, a low rumble growing louder and deeper as they approached, and soon they could see the top of the massive metal structure gleaming in the sun.

When they got there, they passed the rows of rubber-clad poles and walked up to the fence. They gazed through the door that appeared forced and into the building.

"Wonder what it looks like in there?" Benjamin said.

"Probably just a bunch of wires," Nils replied.

"Should we try to get in?"

"No," said Nils. "It could be dangerous."

They stood side by side at the fence, their hands on the metal mesh. "I got a shock once," Benjamin said. "I asked Dad what it was like, and he took out one of those rectangular batteries, and then he told me to lick it."

"What was it like?" Pierre asked.

"It stung my tongue and I couldn't talk for a while. But then it passed."

"But you can get much worse shocks than that," Nils said. "Like if you stick a fork in an electrical outlet. That can kill you."

Benjamin tested the handle on the gate. Just like that, it opened. "Someone broke in here too!" he cried.

He walked through the gate and across the patch of grass in front of the building, stood opposite his brothers and grabbed the fence with one hand. "Let me out!" he cried, pretending to sob. "I beg of you!"

Benjamin looked down at Molly, who was still in his arms, and gently placed a hand on her head. He turned back to his brothers, contorted his face, and held the dog out to them.

"At least take Molly," he moaned. "Let her go free, she doesn't deserve this!"

Pierre giggled.

"Let's head back," said Nils.

"Hold on," said Benjamin. "I just have to see what it looks like in there."

He took a few steps toward the building and stood in the doorway. He peered in but could see only vague shapes. Running his hand along the inside wall, he found a switch and flipped it, and suddenly the whole room was lit up by a fixture on the ceiling. The room was smaller than he'd expected. A little area to stand in, and, on the back wall, a dense row of thick black cables that ran from floor to ceiling. It was like the room was vibrating with the current that ran along the walls, intense and constant, a sound that reminded him of the three big clothes dryers in the basement back home in the city.

"Do you think there's a current in them?" Benjamin called to his brothers.

"Yes!" Nils answered. "Don't touch anything in there."

Benjamin picked up a rock and cautiously tossed it at the cables.

The rock fell to the floor, and nothing happened. He picked up a bigger rock and threw that.

"It doesn't seem like there's any current," he called. "Nothing happens when I throw rocks at it."

"Rocks don't conduct electricity!" Nils called. "That doesn't mean those cables don't!"

Benjamin slowly moved closer to the lines, was now only a foot and a half away from them. He raised his hand toward the black wall.

"Don't touch those!" Nils cried. "I'm serious. You could die!"

"No, no," Benjamin called back. "I'm not going touch anything."

He brought his hand closer and heard a crackling sound from the cable, like static, but it went away as soon as he lowered his hand.

He raised his hand again. Teeny, tiny sparks, almost invisible, appeared between the cable and his hand. The closer he moved, the more it crackled. He'd never heard a sound like it in his life. It reminded him of the sound you heard in movies when they were measuring radioactivity after a big accident. He could control the sound with his hand, making it come closer or move away, and now that he understood the power here, he realized Nils was probably right. If he were to touch the cables he would be gravely injured, and a thought flew through his mind: This is the closest I've ever been to death. He turned around to look at his brothers.

"Do you see this?" he called. He looked up and watched the little flecks of fire zoom out into the room.

"It's sparks! It's like magic!"

"Stop!" Nils shouted. "Stop that right this instant!"

Benjamin raised and lowered his hand, listening to the sound that came and went, the sparks rising around him, and he smiled and looked his brothers in the eye and then the whole room went blue.

He awoke pure. For the first few seconds he was weightless and free. He sat up, trying to orient himself. Then came the pain—fire in his back and down his arms, and reality crashed down on top of him. He looked out at the fence.

He thought: Where are my brothers?

He looked up at the sky, saw that the sun was lower. How long had he been lying there? He tried to get up but his legs wouldn't hold him, so he gave up and sat down again, and then it dawned on him, beginning with a faint shiver that ran through his body.

Molly.

She was lying just a few yards away from him. There was no mistaking it. Her scorched skin and unnatural position. He crawled over to her, lifted her ruined body, and placed it in his lap. He looked at Molly's lifeless face, her half-open mouth, as if she were deeply asleep and would wake up if you shook her a little bit. But he didn't dare do it because he didn't want to touch her wounds, afraid it would hurt her. He pressed her to his chest, to the spot where she had been resting when she died. His breathing came faster and heavier and he heard unfamiliar sounds, realized they were coming from him. And bit by bit, the world vanished. All his life he had battled this feeling, of losing his grip on reality. He had always sought out real places or things to hold tight to, but for the first time he wanted the opposite: to let go of everything that kept him here. He sat in the dark and looked out at the green rectangle of reality outside, and he squeezed his eyes shut and looked at the doorway again and hoped it would soon make itself inaccessible, just go dark, and he would be gone, untethered from reality, caught in darkness forever.

He must have lost consciousness, because when he looked up again the sun was even lower in the sky. He got up and staggered toward the door. His first steps into the light. He passed the fence. The thought: Where are my brothers?

He walked through the forest with the dog in his arms. He couldn't remember how he did it, how he made it home. But he remembered seeing the lake, which was dark; he remembered that it was smooth, no wind. He remembered walking on legs that could hardly bear him and he remembered seeing Mom on the stone steps, standing in her robe. He remembered that Mom's contours were diffuse, that the foliage around the house was fogged over by his tears. He remembered that Mom took a few steps onto the lawn, that she was looking at him with some sort of astonishment. And he remembered that she collapsed on the grass and that she cried out in despair, and that the lake responded.

13

12:00 NOON

The moose fencing ends here; the county highway narrows and its condition worsens, patched asphalt and unexpected dips and dead animals in the road, bloody fur and meat flattened on the pavement. No cars from the opposite direction, only the occasional silver semi hauling timber. Station after station fades out on the car radio. They're on the other side of Sweden, heading deeper and deeper into the forest, and they speak less and less, and by the time they finally turn off the county highway they're not talking at all. They're back on the gravel road; three more miles through the forest and they'll arrive. The rearview mirror vibrates, and he can see the dust rising behind them like smoke from a Bengal flare, billowing out on either side of the car, up over the trees, the spruces getting taller and taller the closer they get to the cottage.

He drives cautiously down the old gravel road, and he sees Nils in the back seat, suddenly leaning forward in concentration, his eyes fixed ahead. It's as though the place has been under the protection of some secret benefactor who has put all their effort into making sure that everything remains untouched in case the family should ever return. The road is grooved and the car gives a shudder in the same spot as always. The pull-out signs on the shoulder still lean at the same angles as they did before. Have days and years even passed here? Or has everything stood still? Maybe something happens to time in the woods, and it doesn't act as it should. Time is a gravel road; if you keep to the right you can watch yourself pass on the other side. He suddenly sees the old Volvo 245 coming at him, Mom and Dad in front, dressed up for Midsummer. And there, in the middle of the back seat, he sees himself, his attentive gaze as he tries to make sure everything goes smoothly.

And now Benjamin can hear the sound of an engine through his open window and suddenly Nils comes over the rise on his moped, its gas tank gleaming in the sun, and he passes quickly, sad and alone, driving fast down the narrow strip of gravel that links their cottage with reality, on his way back from his shift at the grocery store. And look, there among the trees, Benjamin and Pierre running close on each other's heels, lost in the woods; scared and intent, they follow the sound of the moped to find their way home.

The car is approaching the hill where the sunlight always makes it hard to see in the evening, and once he's crested its top he can see himself again. He's standing right at the side of the road, a little boy with skinny legs, in shorts and no shirt. Mom has been off in the city to work for a few days, and Benjamin has gone up to the gravel road on his own to greet her. The boy's clear-eyed gaze meets Benjamin's own as he passes, staring into a stranger's face, uninterested, and then he turns back toward the hill, watching for his mother.

There they go, one by one, all the boys that were him.

Benjamin and his brothers are close now; they turn onto the little tractor path. He remembers the last morning they spent here, a week after the accident. The boys were informed of the decision suddenly, at breakfast: We're going home. Everything became urgent. Big suitcases split open on the living room floor. Dad walked around turning off lights and radiators. As he packed the last few things into the car and checked the doors to make sure they were locked, Mom lit a cigarette and leaned against the hood of the car. She smoked absentmindedly, her eyes on the lake. Benjamin approached her, made an attempt to pick up the purse she had set at her feet, but she waved him off and Benjamin lingered by her side, right next to her. Mom glanced down at Benjamin and back to the lake.

"The day it happened," Mom said, tapping her cigarette with her index finger. "I woke up in the afternoon and couldn't get back to sleep. I was lying in bed, doing a crossword . . ."

She made a gesture, pointed at the sky.

"Suddenly the light went out. I looked up, surprised. What was going on? And then, after just a few seconds, it came back on again."

Mom shook her head slowly.

"I didn't think anything of it at the time, but now I understand."

She smiled.

"We can choose to see it as a beautiful thing. It was like a little greeting, a farewell. The lights went out, and then she was gone."

Mom walked to the barn and stubbed her cigarette out against the wall and stuck the half-smoked butt back in the pack. Then she got in the car.

It's obvious that no one has driven here for a very long time. The grass has grown tall between the tire tracks; bushes strike the undercarriage and smack the car on both sides. Another car approaches on the narrow slope, the old Volvo 245 again, packed to the gills, just like when the family left the cottage on that last day. He sees Dad at the wheel, Mom, beside him, gazing vacantly at the road ahead. In the back are the three brothers, squished close, shoulder to shoulder. Benjamin keeps to the right to leave room for the vehicle to pass. He sees himself for an instant, just a glimpse of the boy in the middle. His sad, alert eyes keeping close watch over everything that happens inside the car and out. The Volvo passes Benjamin and drives up the hill and he watches it in the rearview mirror until it's out of sight. He rounds the last curve and soon the red wooden house emerges from among the trees. He sees the overgrown lot, glances up over the impressive firs, which make the place seem so small. The tall grass rustles under the car. He drives all the way up to the root cellar and turns off the engine. The brothers sit in the car for a moment and look out.

They're back.

2

BEYOND THE
GRAVEL ROAD

14

10:00 A.M.

He looks up at the massive electrical poles along the European highway. Their black cables swoop slowly into the summer outside the car windows, then curve up again, reaching their highest point at the tops of the enormous steel structures that line the road, one hundred yards, then they dip again, curtsying at the meadows below.

One time Benjamin's circuit-breaker box caught fire. He managed to put the flames out, but an electrician had to come fix the short circuit. The man stood in the hall and unscrewed the panel to get access. He was skilled, had the first housing off in just a few seconds, gathered the screws in his beefy fist. He was about to move on, starting on the next housing, when all of a sudden a cross breeze caught the kitchen door and slammed it right behind him, and the electrician's immediate reaction: he dropped everything he was holding and raised his hands as if this were a stick-up. Benjamin was confused. As the electrician gathered up the screws and tools that were scattered across the hall floor, Benjamin asked what had happened. "Occupational hazard," he said. "The instant an electrician hears a bang, he drops everything."

The fear of getting a shock. He never knew it as a child. Before the accident, he was drawn to electricity. Behind the pool complex was a horse farm, and after his swimming lesson one day, as the other children were walking back to school, Benjamin wandered over to the electrical fence that penned the horses into their pasture. He stood there for a long time, looking down at the thin wire and the laminated yellow warning sign that showed a hand touching the line and red lightning bolts flying in all directions. He held both hands close to the wire, as if to dare himself; he cupped his hands without touching it, and then he grabbed on. A quick pulse of current flowed through his hand and reached his armpits before it died out. He recalls feeling strangely exhilarated afterward. It was as if the current had done something about his peculiar lack of energy for a moment; he got a jolt, and as it flowed through him it was as if he heard a voice whispering: "Get moving!"

Pierre is speeding down the highway, always in the left-hand lane. Whenever he has to slow down for someone up ahead—highway tourists passing each other at their own pace—he cruises up right behind them and flashes his brights, immediately scaring them out of the far lane, and Pierre speeds up again and the engine revs as it accelerates, sounding hale and hearty.

"Food!" Pierre suddenly shouts, pointing at a road sign that's approaching from the horizon.

"Finally," Nils mumbles from the back.

The fast-food restaurant looks like any other. The employees wear gold stars on their chests; some have several, others none at all, so everyone can tell who is good and who is bad. Each one wears a name tag, except the oddly young manager, who wanders between registers alert, chicken-like, ashamed of his lazy employees. He walks around, tense, taking over tasks, making things right, sometimes just stopping to gaze at all the guests with a hollow smile.

They order hamburgers and French fries and sit down at one of the tables nearest the exit. Nils takes out his phone.

"I have to deal with the shitstorm you two created," he says. "My guess is that we're wanted by the police."

"Oops," Pierre says with a laugh.

"No, not oops," says Nils. "This is fucking serious."

Nils goes outside and Benjamin watches him walk through the stiff breeze in the parking lot, pressing the phone to one ear and his palm to the other to keep out the racket from the highway. Pierre shakes the French fries onto his hamburger bun, places the little white ketchup packets in a neat line; if one runs out, it's not far to the next.

"I honestly never thought we'd go back," Pierre says.

"No," says Benjamin. A new thought suddenly pops into his mind, and he looks up from his food: "Why not?"

"Because of the accident, I mean," Pierre says. "It was so hard on you." Benjamin watches Pierre make quick work of his food. He dips three fries into the ketchup; they're heavy and droop like tulips as he puts them in his mouth.

"I still don't get it," Pierre says. "Why did you get a shock? Don't you have to touch a line to get shocked? You didn't touch anything."

"I didn't get it either," Benjamin replies. "For ten years I walked around with no idea what had happened. But then I found out."

"So, what happened?" Pierre asks.

And Benjamin tells Pierre about arcing. There are places where an electrical current is so strong that even the air is charged. It heats up to several thousand degrees, until it's so hot that there's a discharge, which acts like a bolt of lightning.

"That's what happened to you?" Pierre asks.

"Yes. I'm lucky to be alive, according to the electricians I told about it."

"You've talked to electricians?"

"Yeah. Lots of them."

"Why?"

"I wanted to understand what had happened to me."

Pierre shakes his head, gazes out at Nils, who has moved and is now standing, with his phone, on a grassy berm that faces the eight-lane highway.

"Do you know how many electrical shocks are reported to the Electrical Safety Board each year?" Benjamin asks. "Fifty. But do you know how many people they think actually get shocked? Over twenty thousand. But no one reports them. Know why?"

"Shame?"

"Exactly. They're ashamed. Because they're electricians. They're supposed to know what they're doing."

"Incredible," Pierre says, putting down his hamburger,

which is nibbled at the edges as if by a rat. He picks up a fry, gnawing at it like it's a pretzel stick, and deposits the end he'd been holding onto a napkin on the table. Benjamin notices that he's left a number of little stumps next to each other.

"Why aren't you eating the ends?" Benjamin asks.

"They're disgusting," he says. "My fingers are dirty—they've been everywhere."

Benjamin watches Pierre as he discards one fry end after the next, and suddenly he feels a wave of tenderness for his brother, because as the little pile grows on the table he thinks he sees a sign that Pierre, too, has got some baggage; that kind of quirk carries a story as well. Benjamin has always been astounded that Pierre seems to have come totally unscathed through childhood. He appears unaffected, as if he simply shook off everything that happened—or maybe it even made him stronger? But as Benjamin watches his brother stack his fries, it's the first time he feels like there might be a trace of something else, because in some way a man who doesn't want to put something in his mouth after touching it wants nothing to do with himself.

The noise of the restaurant is amplified in the silence that ensues. The clattering of machines shaking ice into paper cups, arrhythmic and anxious. A hand dryer turning on and off in the restrooms. The hum of the highway each time another guest comes in. One customer orders a soft serve and a small motor starts up, a deep tone like the lowest note on a piano, and once again he's flung back to the substation, standing in front of the wall of current. He tries at once to rid himself of the images, and maybe he succeeds for a moment, but he knows they will come back. Each time he hears a loud, unexpected noise he will think of the explosion. Like when he flushes the toilet in an airplane bathroom and the valve closes with a bang. Bright lights have the same effect on him. When he's driving on a highway through winter darkness and sees the sudden flash of oncoming brights, he's momentarily paralyzed, remembering that final second when the room went pale just before the explosion. The cool floor and the damp darkness, waking up and orienting himself, squinting into the light.

For the first time during their conversation Benjamin doesn't avert his gaze when Pierre makes eye contact.

"There's one thing I never understood," Benjamin says. "How could you just leave me there?"

Pierre puts down his soda and presses his fingertips to a napkin, shaking his head and smiling.

"Is that what you think?" he says. "I didn't leave you."

"I woke up and you were gone," Benjamin says. "How else am I supposed to interpret it?"

"So you still don't know what happened? I didn't leave you. I ran toward you. I grabbed hold of you and the instant I touched you, I got a shock too."

"No."

"No?"

"That can't be right," Benjamin says.

"Well, you were unconscious. When you got shocked, you became like a live wire too, and I got a shock from touching you. I just passed out. When I woke up, I saw Nils running off through the forest. I tried to wake you up, but I couldn't. I thought Nils was getting help. So I took off after him. I caught up just as he got back to the cottage. He lay down in the hammock, and I had no idea what was going on."

"So?" Benjamin asked. "What did you do?"

"I screamed at him that we had to go back. But he refused. I panicked, looked for Mom and Dad, but they were nowhere to be found. So I ran back by myself."

"No, that's not true. I woke up alone in the substation."

"I got lost. I ran and ran, trying to find you, until I was all mixed up. I couldn't find you and I couldn't find my way home."

Benjamin brings his fist to his forehead.

"Don't you remember?" Pierre says. "When you got back to the house with Molly, I wasn't there. I was out in the forest looking for you."

Benjamin closes his eyes. Midsummer Eve. He's carried Molly back down to the house. She's lying dead on the lawn in front of the stone steps. Mom picks her up and collapses on the grass with her. She hugs her, she screams.

Nils.

There he is, on the slope down to the lake, keeping his distance, observing in silence. Mom looks up at Benjamin. He remembers minor details, like that there's a string of mucus between her upper and lower lips. That you can see her white breasts through her open robe. "What have you done?" she shouts at Benjamin over and over, shifting between rage and despair. "What have you done?"

But where is Pierre? He tries to see him but can't find him anywhere.

"You weren't there," Benjamin says.

"No. I was running around the forest. At last I gave up and sat down on a rock. Eventually I heard Mom screaming. I'd never heard her sound like that. She was repeating, 'What have you done? What have you done?' And I set off in the direction of her screams. When I got to the house, everything was upside down. It was . . ." He shakes his head. "It was chaos."

"Yeah," Benjamin says, gazing down at the tabletop. "Then what did you do?"

"I don't remember. I do remember that I wanted to wash up. I didn't want Mom and Dad to notice what had happened. I had burns on my hands and arms. Don't you remember, I had burns that lasted weeks?"

"No."

"I went to the bathroom and my skin fell off when I washed my hands. I stood there looking at all the little pieces of skin on the porcelain and heard Mom screaming outside and it was ringing in my ears. It was like I was at war."

"I never knew this," Benjamin says. "I never knew you tried to save me. I didn't know you searched for me."

Pierre shrugs.

"Why didn't you ever tell me this?" Benjamin asks.

"I thought you knew," Pierre says. "And Mom and Dad said you weren't okay and that we shouldn't talk to you about what happened." The images overtake him. Staggering through the forest with Molly, coming to the cottage, seeing the calm lake. He sees Mom on the stone steps. Her half-open mouth, her vacant eyes, the instant before she realizes. But now he can see his little brother too, imagines him in the forest. He's lost and has given up, but then he hears Mom's screams through the pines. There he goes, the little boy, taking off with his burned arms dangling at his sides. There is the seven-year-old, running, the sound of his mother's sorrow guiding him home.

Benjamin and Pierre stand up and put on their jackets.

Pierre brings Nils's hamburger to the car. As they leave the table, Benjamin looks at the leftover pile of fries, the stubs of potato Pierre stacked in a neat pyramid, like a small manifestation of self-hatred.

They get in the car. The freezer meals Nils brought along have thawed and the inside of the car smells vaguely of beef pierogi. They enter the E-highway, which narrows into a country road. The moose fencing ends here; the county highway narrows and its condition worsens, patched asphalt and unexpected dips and dead animals in the road, bloody fur and meat flattened on the pavement. No cars from the opposite direction, only the occasional silver semi hauling timber. Station after station fades out on the car radio. They're on the other side of Sweden, heading deeper and deeper into the forest, and they speak less and less, and by the time they finally turn off the county highway they're not talking at all. They are traveling through the wormhole again.

15

THE GRADUATION PARTY

Dad was standing at the window that faced the square and looking down. He checked his watch, took a seat at the kitchen table, gazed down at his lap. He was dressed up; his flesh-toned loafers had become one with his shins, his suit pants left hanging up in the kitchen until the last minute as always, so the creases would remain intact, a trick that often raised the ire of both Nils and Mom as he walked around the apartment in his underwear for hours before any sort of festivity. He was wearing his own old student cap, faded and shapeless, a yellowed scrap of fabric on his head.

"Shit," he whispered, returning to the window. He had to press his face to the glass to get a glimpse of the street below. Benjamin thought about how Dad would look from the other side, if someone happened to see him from the square: his hands against the pane, his flattened cheek, his wide, searching eyes inspecting the terrain. Like a zoo animal that has just now understood its captivity.

"This is just about unreal," Dad muttered. "How could you be late for your own graduation party?"

The family had gathered that morning in the schoolyard to participate in the traditional greeting of their new graduate Nils as the students ran out of the building. Dad had let Pierre and Benjamin skip school to take part. This was important. Pierre got to hold the sign, a picture of Nils when he was three, in which he was sitting on a potty and smiling at the camera. The picture made Benjamin think of a family anecdote that Mom liked to tell, how Benjamin had once emptied the potty after Pierre was done. Mom had discovered him in the bathroom with a piece of Pierre's poop in his hand; she described how Benjamin had been gnawing on it from the side "as if it was a chicken kabob," and she gave a long and silent laugh, and every time she told this story Benjamin left the room.

Rain began to fall on the schoolyard and the family crowded under a big umbrella. Then some hype man, maybe the headmaster, took a megaphone and counted down from ten and the doors opened and the students poured into the small asphalt yard, all running around in confusion and looking for their families. All but Nils. Benjamin spotted him right away, smiling, walking calmly and steadily straight for the photograph of himself on the potty.

"Bravo," Mom cried, raising her fist tentatively as he approached. She and Dad embraced Nils. He had sprigs of flowers, teddy bears, and tiny champagne bottles on blue-and-yellow ribbons around his neck, front-heavy with other people's love, proof of his entire cohort hanging against his chest, friendships Benjamin only ever caught quick glimpses of at home in their apartment. Nils often had classmates with him when he came home each afternoon, sometimes four or five guys tumbling into the entryway and roughhousing down the hall. Nils quickly herded them into his room and closed the door, but Benjamin observed them closely as they went by, these colossal humans, their faces erupting with pimples, quiet and long-legged, thighs up to their rib cages.

Nils was carrying the brown envelope containing his grades. An atomic bomb of disappointment detonated silently in the schoolyard when Dad slit it open and eyed the results. He handed the piece of paper to Mom, reading it once more over her shoulder, nodding as if this was more or less what he'd expected. He folded the paper and stuck it in his inner pocket. But Benjamin saw the discouragement in their eyes. There had been portents of this all spring, that Nils's grades might not be as spectacular as Mom had always led the other brothers to believe. Nils quickly said good-bye again, because he would be riding around on the back of a truck with his classmates for the parade through town. He promised to come home as soon as he could, and then there was a mild commotion, he ran into a friend and they hugged and the champagne bottles around their necks clattered together. They wandered off with their arms around each other's shoulders, heading for the long line of idling trucks, decorated with leafy birch branches and sheets hanging down the sides, spray-painted with cheeky messages. Dad called out as his son vanished into the throngs: "We'll be waiting for you at home!"

And Mom lit a cigarette and they walked back home, all under the umbrella, through the tunnel under the commuter train tracks, up to the main street, the small family with their sign in the air, like a tiny demonstration crossing the square.

That was over two hours ago now, and since then Dad had been darting back and forth to the window in hopes of catching a glimpse of his missing son. He went to the sideboard and checked on the food. There were some platters with a few slices of mortadella and salted radishes. Four deviled eggs with lumpfish caviar on top. And, on its very own platter—Finnish Emmentaler cheese. This was the centerpiece of the party, what Nils loved most of all. He liked to cut a slice and spread a thick layer of butter on it, then roll the cheese into a tube and eat it in one bite in front of the TV in the evenings. Pierre and Benjamin couldn't bear to watch, fatty butter on the fatty cheese; they pretended to gag and pointedly left the living room each time he started. And Nils sat there in the dark, in the cold light of the television, slicing his cheese down to nothing.

Mom was curled up on the sofa, smoking, the ashtray in her lap so she didn't have to lean over the table. She was reading a magazine, and when Dad fumbled the silverware and dropped a fork on the floor, she looked up.

"Put the champagne in the fridge—it must be warm by now," she said, going back to her magazine.

Down on the square came sudden music as one of the trucks full of students crept by, and Dad hurried to the window, pressing up close. "Shit," Dad hissed as the truck moved out of sight, and he changed position. Benjamin heard the sound of the elevator stopping on their floor and the doors opening, the jingle of a key ring approaching their apartment door.

"Here he comes," Benjamin said.

"No, no," Dad said, staring out. "That's not his truck."

The door opened. "Hello," Nils called.

Dad rushed to the door.

"Welcome!" he cried, looking around. "Benjamin," he whispered, gesturing at him to come greet his brother, and then he turned back and roared at his other son—"Pierre!"—who immediately appeared in the door of his room.

"Sorry," Nils said. "The truck went all the way into the city and I couldn't jump off."

"It's fine," Dad said. He fingered the bottle of champagne, peeling back the foil like a rose and twisting the cork with a grimace, holding it away from himself in case it shot up at the ceiling.

"Pink champagne!" he called.

The five of them gathered in the middle of the living room and watched as Dad filled three flutes. He took his glasses off and tapped them gently against the rim of his flute. He cleared his throat.

"To our wonderful graduate," he said, raising his glass. "We're so proud of you."

Mom, Dad, and Nils clinked their glasses and drank.

"It's warm," Mom said, turning to Benjamin. "Would you grab us some ice?"

When Pierre grabbed a plate and took a deviled egg, Dad hissed at him: "Honestly. Let Nils go first, for God's sake."

"It's okay," Nils said, his friendly tone both unfamiliar and affected. "He can go first."

Fifteen minutes later, Nils got ready to leave again. He was supposed to meet some friends, and then he would spend the evening going to parties. He stood in the hall, bent over his shoes, Dad by the entrance to the kitchen.

"Nils," he called. He waved the Emmentaler. "Look what you missed."

"Ooh," Nils said. "Yum."

"We can have it tonight when you get home. It's your last night, after all."

"It's a deal," Nils replied.

The door banged shut and Nils was gone. Dad stood there for a moment, looking at the door. He took off his student cap and placed it on the hall table. He went to his room. And so began another waiting period, for Nils to come home again. Each hour was important, because tomorrow he would leave for his trip, nine months as a volunteer in Central America. Benjamin took the fact that it was happening so swiftly, right after his graduation, as a dangerous provocation of Mom and Dad, a way to demonstrate that he didn't want to live at home a day more than was necessary. But Mom and Dad seemed to believe him when he said he needed a break from it all, that he wanted to clear his mind and see the world. Benjamin walked down the hall that led to their bedrooms and cautiously opened the door to Nils's room. His bags were already packed, three suitcases piled one on top of another. His CD rack was empty, as was the bookcase. All that was left on the walls were the symmetrical grease stains from the tacky putty that had once held up Nils's movie posters. It was clinically done. Nils had said he would come home again in the spring, but Benjamin knew that someone who left a room in this condition, so thoroughly purged, was leaving for good.

He went to his own room. It was afternoon, but it felt like

evening. Mom was back on the sofa with her magazine. Dad was in an easy chair in his study, reading a book. Benjamin lay on his bed; he closed his eyes for a while and fell asleep. When he woke up, it was dark out. He looked at the clock radio: 10:12. He was cold, thanks to an open window, and he thought about getting up but he couldn't quite bring himself to. He listened for sounds in the apartment. The TV was on in the living room, but he couldn't hear any talking. Had Nils come home? Suddenly he heard Mom's shrill voice:

"Would you just quit that?!"

Probably Pierre chewing on ice cubes—Mom hated that, and Pierre knew it but couldn't stop. Benjamin heard steps on the parquet, Pierre leaving the living room and going to his own room. Pierre came back out again, Benjamin heard the steps, and suddenly he was standing in the doorway of Benjamin's room. He walked right in, held up the cigarette between his fingers, and stepped out onto the little balcony outside Benjamin's room. Pierre had been secretly smoking for some time and was constantly growing bolder. Mom smelled his fingers sometimes, doing spot checks, and to keep from being found out Pierre put drops of vinegar on his hands after each cigarette. He always carried a bottle in his bag, and he scrubbed up in the elevator before he came home at night. Always that sharp odor in the stairwell, on his clothes. Mom never caught on, but she once remarked, puzzled, that it smelled like "food" when she went into his room.

Benjamin watched Pierre out there on the balcony, his dexterous handling of the cigarette, his hand cupped so the match wouldn't blow out in the breeze, how he could let the lit cigarette dangle from his lips like it was no big deal as he pulled up the zipper on his jacket, how he rested his arms on the railing, sucking in and blowing out smoke through his nose. He moved like a much older man sometimes, like when his gaze seemed to freeze as if he had suddenly thought of one of life's sorrows, or when he stared out at the high-rises, his face wry after taking yet another drag. Benjamin no longer thought Pierre looked like a kid or a teenager; he seemed weighed down the way only someone with a lot of life experience could be. He was increasingly closed off, seldom wanted to talk about things that they'd gone through together. This was a change. Benjamin recalled one time when Mom and Dad were having a bad fight, shouting at each other in the apartment, it escalated and got physical, quick steps across the hall, yanking on a door, Mom trying to get away from Dad's fury. He remembered Dad's wild grin as he tore the door open, got a hand in the gap and lashed out. He remembered pulling Pierre into a closet and closing the door as the fight raged on outside, the sounds of bodies, shouting, sounds that fed unthinkable images into Benjamin's mind, and they sat on the floor and held each other, Pierre crying, Benjamin covering Pierre's ears and whispering, "Don't listen."

They were together.

There were still moments when he experienced flashes of what they could be. Early mornings in the kitchen, standing next to each other in their pajamas and squeezing chocolate syrup into their milk. And when Pierre spilled, Benjamin would imitate Dad and whisper in horror: "You're clumsy!" And Pierre imitated Mom's method of resolving conflicts: "I'm going to bed." They tittered. There they stood with their morning hair, quiet again, stirring their chocolate milk; they were together.

But then they went to school and Pierre was a different person there. The two boys might pass each other without so much as a greeting. During breaks, between classes, in the hall, Benjamin would suddenly hear a scuffle among the rows of lockers, and when he walked by he would see that Pierre had shoved a student up against the wall, saw him leaning over to press his forehead against the younger boy's. He took only very brief note of this as he passed, didn't want to look, but then he carried the image of his brother's explosive nature inside him; he couldn't forget it. He had seen it in the guys down at the youth center, and in the gangs that roved around the square and sometimes got on the subway and paralyzed an entire car. In them he saw a type of masculinity he couldn't comprehend and wasn't a part of. Now he was slowly beginning to understand that it was in his family too, in Pierre, in his increasingly irrational behavior, in how his bag clattered with throwing stars he'd made in woodshop class. And Benjamin had seen him smoking behind the gym in the afternoons, throwing stars at the wall with his friends. One day he bleached his hair, all on his own, without asking Mom. Something must have gone wrong, because it turned bright yellow, and he dyed it back the next day, so black it was almost purple. It was just hair, but it affected the way people perceived him. That inconceivably dark hair, which could be spotted from the other side of the schoolyard, and his guarded gaze, as if he were always about to walk into an ambush. And that constant sound in the halls, the clatter of throwing stars in his bag, and of younger kids being shoved up against lockers.

He began to watch Pierre in secret on breaks, and only then, in studying his brother from a distance, did he see himself. It was midwinter, below freezing and dark by the two o'clock break. The students played four square on the icy asphalt and steam came from their mouths and when the kids tried to throw the tennis ball it stuck to their snow-matted mittens. Benjamin spotted Pierre on the fringes of the game, looking on in his very thin jacket, no hat, his red hands shoved into the pockets of his jeans. And a sudden rage came over Benjamin: Why hadn't Mom and Dad given him a warmer coat? Why didn't he have a hat or mittens?

Only on his way back to class did he notice that he was freezing too, and that his jacket was just as flimsy as his brother's. He slowly put all the clues together, and he learned to know himself by looking around him. The filth at home, the flecks of urine on the floor around the toilet, making it crunch when Dad walked there in his slippers, the dust bunnies under the beds, swirling about gently in the breeze from the open window. The sheets slowly yellowing in the children's beds until they were finally changed. All the dirty dishes in the sink; when you turned on the faucet the fruit flies flew up, roused from their hiding places between the plates. The rings of dirt in the bathtub like tidewater marks in the harbor, the garbage bags piling up one on top of another next to the shoe rack in the hall.

Benjamin began to realize that not only was their home dirty, so were the people in it. He began to put the puzzle pieces together, comparing himself to others. During class he would clean the rind of dirt under his nails with the help of a mechanical pencil. It helped pass the time, and he liked that the task gave immediate results. He gently dragged the metal under each nail and the dark streaks disappeared without a trace, one after the next. He gathered the grime in a little pile on his desk. But when he happened to glance at the fingernails of his classmates, he never saw any dirt; someone took care of their hands, made sure they were clean, that their fingernails were clipped. The art teacher, who often leaned over him, smelled of the coffee on his breath, and some kind of apple-scented detergent that lingered in the knitted sweaters he wore. One time he asked Benjamin to stay behind after class. The teacher squatted down beside Benjamin's desk and said that sometimes when he was helping him he noticed that Benjamin smelled like sweat, and he didn't want to interfere but he knew how teenagers were, they took every opportunity to be cruel to each other, and one day they would tease him because of his body odor. Benjamin listened carefully to his art teacher. There are really just two things to remember, he said: Change your socks and your underwear every day. Shower every morning. That evening Benjamin took stock of his hygiene. When no one was looking, he stuck his hand inside his shirt, wiped his armpit, and smelled his fingers. For the first time, he smelled his own sweat. Suddenly he could see clearly.

On the balcony outside, Pierre made one last gesture with his cigarette and flicked it away with his thumb and middle finger; it flew off like a firefly over the railing. He came in, quietly closing the balcony door behind him, took a few steps through the room, and then he was gone. The smell of vinegar lingered in Benjamin's room after he left.

Benjamin remained in bed. The lights in the parking lot flickered and came to life one by one, shining through the blinds and forming narrow spears of light on the wall. A small lamp on the windowsill emitted a faint glow that appeared as dots on the ceiling; they looked like the luminous jellyfish in a green sea he'd once seen on a nature show on TV.

He listened to the sounds of the suburban night, two dogs barking hysterically at each other below. A few young guys ran across the square, trying to catch the subway; he heard them laughing. And, fainter but mightier, the distant roar of the big highway half a mile or so away. He should get up. The whole afternoon and evening had passed. He was tired, wanted to sleep, but there must be something wrong with someone who sleeps so much. He sat up in bed, slowly stood up, felt cold, went to the closet to get a sweater. On the other side of the door he heard Dad getting ready for bed. Dad always took his preparations with him into the hall, brushing his teeth there as if he didn't want to miss anything that might happen. Then he went to the little lavatory next to the big bathroom, and only when he discovered that his visit to the toilet was making loud noises did he close the door, firmly and kind of irritated, as if someone else had left it open. He spat a few times into the sink, ran the tap, and then he was done. His heavy footfalls in the hall. Through his half-open door Benjamin saw him go by in his pajamas. Dad stopped and looked down at the floor.

"Good night!" he called to the apartment.

"Good night," Mom replied from the living room.

Dad lingered for a moment; it seemed like he was trying to find something in her tone, something to suggest that she wanted to stay up with him for a while after all, have a sandwich and a nip. But her response was curt and decisive, and he must have understood that it wasn't going to happen this time. Benjamin heard him go into his bedroom. They'd been sleeping in separate rooms for a few years—Mom claimed it was because Dad snored so loudly. And Benjamin lay there in the dark, following along with the familiar, recurring sounds. He heard Mom turn down the volume of the TV immediately, saw the living room go dark as she turned out light after light. Mom always did this once Dad went to bed, because she knew that he might not be able to sleep and after half an hour he would get up and open the bedroom door and greedily peer out, on the hunt for company, and the instant that happened she turned off the TV, quick as a wink, so the living room was pitch black. Dad never went all the way to the living room; he stopped after a few steps into the hall. And then he went back to bed. Mom sat in the dark for a minute. Then she turned on the TV again.

Benjamin woke up. He was in bed but didn't remember returning to it. And he must have fallen asleep. He leaned over to look at the clock radio: 12:12. He heard the elevator come to life and pictured the lonely little iron cube climbing through the darkness, hoisted through its shaft. He liked to lie here at night, listening to it work its way through the building; he knew all its sounds, the click when the locking mechanism secured the door and it began to move, the goofy chatter of the bell when someone accidentally hit the alarm, the little thud as the elevator arrived at a floor and finally stopped. He knew it was Nils coming home, and he was struck by the realization that this was the last time he would hear the familiar sound of Nils in the elevator, his quiet footfalls between the elevator and the apartment door, the jangle of his keys, which always started before he got out of the elevator, a typical manifestation of his rational nature: he wanted to be ready, didn't want to waste any time standing outside the door and digging for his keys. The door opened and closed. Benjamin could see his brother in the yellow light beyond his door. He was glowing, shiny from the world outside, from the back of the truck on the gray June evening, chilly outdoor parties with lukewarm beer, from making out in bushes, echoey train platforms and crowded red buses streaming out into the suburbs. He stood there in his glow, unreachable, already gone, a legend who'd once lived in this house. Mom came to greet him and they went to the kitchen. Benjamin could hear only fuzzy bits of their conversation; he heard the fridge open and close, maybe someone got out the Emmentaler cheese? And the scrape of chairs being pulled out as they settled at the kitchen table, the dull murmur through three walls, hard to hear the words being exchanged but impossible to miss their tone, their gentle vowels, tolerant silences. Benjamin became calm, he became sad, he felt his heart beating, he knew he had to get out of bed before the chance passed him by, he had to rush to the kitchen and beg of Nils: Stay. He had to tell him there was no other choice, he had to stay, or else he honestly didn't know what was going to happen. He knew that Nils's departure meant something would be broken once and for all. Because how could he ever repair his family if one of its members disappeared? He also knew that Nils's journey spelled danger for Benjamin himself. If Nils disappeared, that meant someone disappearing from reality, a hand on his shoulder, holding him in place. Now there would be one less person to reassure Benjamin that this family existed and that he existed within it. Someone he could exchange glances with over the dinner table and who could silently affirm him: You exist. And this happened.

He lay there. Felt his back pressing against the mattress. He thought about how far it was to the ground. Third floor. Thirty-five feet down, maybe forty. He wouldn't survive that kind of fall, if the structure were to give way, if he happened to fall right through the concrete. He looked up at the ceiling, searching for something to hold on to, fumbling for sheets and pillows, otherwise he would tumble toward the ceiling, a free fall at sixty miles per hour, straight for the surface of the water, toward the luminous jellyfish.

He had to get up, he had to run out. But how could he do that now, in the middle of a conversation that must not be interrupted under any circumstances? This was his duty, to fix things so his family would talk to each other just like Mom and Nils were doing out there, so that they loved each other and everything was okay. The friendly words came like a hum through the walls, an optimistic crooning, full of love that riveted him to the bed. He heard Nils say something and he heard Mom laugh. And then another sound, a door opening—Dad was up! On one of his tours through the apartment to see if anyone wanted to keep him company for a while. Mom hadn't realized he was awake, because Benjamin still couldn't hear any wrath, any shrill voices in the night; the conversation in the kitchen was still united, calm, intimate. He heard sounds he didn't understand. He heard something rumbling across the parquet and saw the shape of Nils as he passed the crack in the door: he was rolling his suitcases out. Benjamin didn't understand—he wasn't supposed to leave until tomorrow. Weren't they going to eat breakfast together and say good-bye? What was going on?

He looked at the clock: 7:20.

He had to get up!

Dad walked by outside, no longer in pajamas, now fully dressed. "Do you have everything?" he heard Dad say.

"Yeah," said Nils.

Struggling with suitcases, the door opening. Benjamin wanted to scream but couldn't get a word out.

"Good-bye, my boy," said Dad. "Take care of yourself. And call when you can."

The door closed.

16

8:00 A.M.

The sky opens and an insane downpour engulfs the car, and soon after the rain comes the wind. Benjamin can see the signs of it in the sudden darkness, in the pennants tugging at their poles above hotel façades, and in a pedestrian leaning into the storm as he walks down the sidewalk. This is the sort of wind that might blow a city away, a storm that should have a human name.

And as fast as the storm arrived, it passes. The brothers climb out of the car, the air clear after the cloudburst. They cross the cemetery. Dirt has splashed onto the headstones; the water is still flowing away in the ditches. The path is narrow, the dead crowded close on either side of the gravel they're walking on. Benjamin and Nils side by side, Pierre not far behind, reading aloud the names of those who have died. He sometimes informs his brothers of the details, reading the poems carved into the headstones. Those who died young especially capture his attention.

"Twelve years old!" Pierre calls.

He walks with his eyes cast down at the headstones, stops, Benjamin hears him cry out behind them: "Oh shit, here's a seven-year-old!"

Behind a low wall is a gray concrete building—the crematorium. Benjamin visited one like it a long time ago, on a class trip, and there are some things he'll never be able to forget. He saw the refrigeration rooms and the freezer rooms where the coffins were stored before being burned. Dead people in rows, waiting to disappear. The industrial handling, the forklifts that ferried the coffins back and forth. The staff's jargon, gibes and shouts as they transported the bodies, as if they were working at a fruit warehouse. Lined up in the heat, illuminated by the yellow glow of the oven, the children watched as a coffin was fed into the fire. Through a small glass pane they could observe the raging fire as wood, fabric, flesh melted into one, was destroyed. The crematorium operator took out a stainless steel container that looked like the pans they served food out of at school. He had a long shovel that he used to scoop out the human remains. There was a basket right next to the oven where the attendant placed things that the fire hadn't destroyed. Amalgam fillings, nails from the coffin. The children were allowed to peer into the basket; the attendant held it out, shaking it like a bag of candy. Benjamin saw screws that had been in hips, prostheses, the remains of insulin pumps and pacemakers, the knickknacks of death, covered in ash. The man warned the children that it was time to look away if they wanted to, and some of the students turned to look at the wall, but Benjamin watched attentively as the operator raked what was left of the skeleton into a container. Some of the bones were so intact that you could see their shapes. The man used the shovel to separate the largest pieces. Then the container went into a crusher and then, as the fine powder was poured into an urn, it struck Benjamin that it wasn't ash, as he'd always thought. It was crushed bone.

The brothers step through the door of the crematorium; the small anteroom is like a lobby, with an unattended counter. Pierre presses an electronic doorbell and it rings somewhere far off. Benjamin looks around. This is like standing in the middle of a working life and a private life at the same time, it's both an office and a break room, with open almanacs and chewed-on pencils on the counter, a photograph of a hockey team on the wall. A man comes out from the inner parts of the crematorium, and it's obvious from the start that death is handled differently here than at the funeral homes, where slender people dressed in black serve coffee to widows. The man arrives with a jangle of keys, wearing jeans that have only a little color left down the sides.

"We're here for our mother's urn," Nils says, taking a folder from his laptop bag, spreading the papers out on the counter, handing one of them to the man, who starts typing at his computer.

Silence.

"Right," he says. "Yes, here she is. But isn't she supposed to be interred today, this afternoon?"

"No, there's been a change," Nils says. "I called earlier this morning to cancel the interment."

"That's odd," says the man. "I don't have anything about that here."

"I got a confirmation."

The man types at his computer, leaning close to make out the information. A radio is on in the next room, and, farther off, an echoey clatter, like gunshots in a hangar, followed by intense voices. Benjamin imagines a unique problem happening to whoever's back there, a coffin that turns out to be too large for the oven door.

"Who did you speak with when you called?" the man asks. "It wasn't me."

"I don't recall. But it was only a little while ago."

"Really," he says. "This doesn't make any sense."

Nils flips through his documents again, taking out more of them and placing them side by side on the counter.

"Here's the notice to the county administrative board, saying that we intend to bury our mother on our own and that we want to pick up the urn. I filled it in and e-mailed it to them this morning."

The man behind the counter doesn't touch the documents, just leans over to read them.

"This isn't a notice," he says. "It's an application. You have to have it approved by the county administrative board."

"What?"

"You can't just come and get an urn. You have to apply for a private ash-scattering approval. You tell them where you want to scatter the ashes and attach a map, or a nautical chart if you want to do it at sea. Then the board reads your application and they typically contact you with their decision after a week or so."

"Unfortunately, we don't have a week. This has to happen today."

"I can't give you the urn unless I know the arrangements have been approved by the board."

"Can't you just look at these forms? You can see there's no funny business. It's just that we're a little pressed for time."

"We have a saying around here," the man says, gathering the documents and placing them in one pile. "'Everything has its time, and one thing at a time.' You can't be in a hurry when you do this sort of work."

Nils gives an abrupt laugh. He methodically puts the papers back in his folder and closes it.

"Here's the deal. Our mother was supposed to be buried today. And last night my brothers and I were at her apartment, to see if there was anything valuable there we wanted to have, before the movers came to throw it all out. In her top desk drawer we found a letter that said *If I die*."

Nils opens the folder again and takes out an envelope. He hands it to the man.

"You don't have to read it all, but here." He points at the final paragraph.

"Right there, our mother says, plain and simple, that she doesn't want to be buried here. Which means she doesn't want the funeral I've been planning full-time for the last two weeks. No one would be happier than me to bury her here this afternoon, but we're just trying to comply with our mother's last wishes. So we have to stop the interment today. And we have to get the urn."

The man's lips move silently as he reads.

"Wow," he says. "I can see how this is disrupting your plans."

"Yes," Nils says. "It's been a long night."

"I can imagine," says the man. He hands the letter back to Nils. "But I'm sorry. It's against the law for me to give you the urn."

He rests his hands on the counter. His rolled-up sleeves reveal old tattoos, their edges blurred into his skin.

"It's a matter of respect for the dead," the man says.

The room is quiet. Nils looks down at his folder. Pierre steps forward and stops next to the desk, directly in front of the man. Benjamin sees it right away, in Pierre's posture, his neck receding into his shoulders, his voice far back in his throat, almost like he's choking up.

"Could we at least look at the urn for a minute?"

"Sure," says the man. "I don't see why not."

"Where is it?"

"In the urn room. Hold on."

The man searches on his computer, muttering a few numbers to himself to memorize them, and walks off; Benjamin hears the jangle of keys in some back room, and after a moment he returns. The urn is green, made of copper. Smooth and round, with a little knob in the shape of a torch on the top. The man places the urn on the counter, and then everything happens very fast. Pierre grabs the urn and hands it to Benjamin, charges the counter and leaps it, knocks the man to the floor, and gets on top of him.

"You little rat," he says.

The man squirms and grimaces, trying to fight his way free, but Pierre's grip is strong, and he presses his arm to the man's neck.

"For fuck's sake, Pierre," says Nils. He looks at his brother, a quick glance, makes up his mind, takes the folder, turns toward the door, and heads that way. "Madhouse," he says to himself, and then he's gone. Benjamin's feet are riveted to the floor. He watches Nils leave the room and can't follow; he sees Pierre attacking the crematorium guy and can't interfere. He can only stand there and watch the inexplicable events unfolding. He looks at Pierre's rage. He doesn't know what it means, he can't feel the breadth of its power, doesn't know what Pierre is capable of now. Pierre has a knee in the man's back and leans over, whispering in his ear:

"Our mother is dead."

"Let me go!" the man cries.

"Shut up!" Pierre hisses. "Our mother just died. And you're saying we have no right to her ashes?"

Pierre must have him in a hold that's twisting one of his joints, because the man lies still, his face pressed to the floor. After a moment, the man gives up; soon he's perfectly motionless.

"I'm going to let you go in a second," Pierre says, "and you're going to stay right where you are. Do you understand? You aren't going to move an inch, because otherwise I'll hurt you again."

Slowly, Pierre loosens his grip. He gets up. The man stays on the floor.

"You rat," Pierre says. He jumps back over the counter. "Come on, Benjamin."

Pierre takes the urn from Benjamin and the brothers leave, hurrying down the gravel path, past the gravestones. Benjamin sees the car, all the drops of rain on its paint; it's parked sloppily on the narrow road, its right-hand set of tires on the pavement, its left-hand ones on hallowed ground. Pierre opens the trunk and places the urn inside. Benjamin passes Nils, who's in the back seat, notices how he's staring at the cement-colored sky. They get in and drive off.

"What are we going to do about Dad's grave?" Benjamin asks.

"We don't have time for that right now, because they could very well come after us," Pierre says. "But I can drive past it on the way out."

Benjamin picks up the bouquet of tulips he'd set on the dashboard, fingers their rough stems. Dad and Mom loved tulips, because they were a sign of spring. Each Friday between March and May, as far back as he can remember, Dad had bought a bouquet of tulips; they stood on the kitchen table, waiting for her when she got home from work. There's the tallest birch in the cemetery, and under it is Dad. It had always been the plan, that his spot would be there. The brothers roll by the tree slowly, look at Dad's gravestone, a sturdy block with the few symbols that sum up his life. "See the hole?" Pierre says.

Beside Dad's grave is a cylindrical hole in the ground. Just the right size for an urn. The caretaker has done his job; everything is ready for this afternoon, when Mom was supposed to be lowered into the ground there. Fog is creeping in from the forest, the heavy birch dips its leaves to the ground around the site, and Benjamin remembers something from a lifetime ago, in Mom and Dad's bedroom, boxes piled along the wall—they've just moved in? Mom and Dad are taking things from the boxes and suddenly they rush to the bare bed, laughter and competition, because both of them want the same side, both of them want to lie on the right. They shout and play-fight, rolling around, and then they kiss. Nils is embarrassed and disappears, but Benjamin stays put, he doesn't want to miss a thing. When Benjamin looks over at Dad's gravestone he sees that she would have gotten the right side, and they would lie there being dead together, but Mom's letter changed everything, and in a few hours the caretaker will come back with new information and fill in the hole, consummating Mom's betrayal, rendering Dad's loneliness eternal.

THEY TURN OUT of the cemetery, and soon they're on their way, a car loaded with the brothers and a copper container full of their mother's crushed bones. They drive through the suburbs, through the outer-ring communities, so many red lights, and out to the highway. He looks up at the massive electrical poles along the European highway. Their black cables swoop slowly into the summer outside the car windows, then curve up again, reaching their highest point at the tops of the enormous steel structures that line the road, one hundred yards, then they dip again, curtsying at the meadows below.

17

THE ESCAPEES

The day began with the promise of a ski trip. It was a Sunday in March, two weeks after Benjamin's twentieth birthday. He was sitting in the kitchen, watching as Dad made himself breakfast. Dad was wearing the pale robe that so unforgivingly displayed the various stains of breakfasts past, his hair was every which way, his glasses hanging by their cord on his chest. He muttered "Damn" to himself as he dropped an egg too hard into the boiling water and it cracked. He was torn between tasks when the toast popped up just as the kettle began to whistle, but he sorted things and took his tray to the tiny balcony outside Benjamin's room. Benjamin followed close behind. Fresh, cold air and sunshine that brought warmth only when the faint breeze abated. It was too chilly to sit outside, but Dad didn't care, he always said he didn't want to miss spring.

"You face the sun," said Dad. "It's so nice."

"No, I want you to."

"Are you sure?" Dad asked.

He remembers sitting out there when the other family members were asleep, watching the morning come into sharper focus. Dad drank his tea, which smelled like tar and poison and steamed in the cold. He gazed out at the snow-covered parking lot, and the woods just past that, encircling the lake. He remembers Dad closing his eyes for a moment and leaning his head back against the building, and that each time Dad opened up a new egg to peel it, he could tell the direction of the wind when the steam disappeared against the façade.

"Should we do something today, just you and me?" Dad asked.

"Sure. Like what?"

"I don't know," Dad said. "Shall we go cross-country skiing?"

Benjamin looked at his dad, puzzled. "Cross-country skiing? Do we have skis?"

"Yes, of course. They must still be around. I think they're in the basement somewhere."

It felt like a different life, but he and Dad used to go skiing together when Benjamin was little. White tracks through black forests, up over vast expanses with views over valleys where Dad was so moved that he had to just stand there for a moment and look. They got out their bag lunches, double rye sandwiches with caviar that had squished out at the edges, sticking to the plastic wrap, and oranges they peeled with frozen fingers. And then they kept moving, the sun low and diamond sparkles on the snow, fast down the hills, into the forest, which was silent, deserted, and dead, but there were marks of claws and hooves over the ski tracks, as if the forest lived a secret life when no one could see it, and they came home with rosy cheeks and lay down on the sofa and Dad rolled Benjamin's feet in his hands as if he were making meatballs, to warm them up again.

"It would be wonderful to go skiing again," Benjamin said.

"Wouldn't it?" Dad said.

"Just you and me," said Benjamin.

"Yes, just you and me," said Dad.

Benjamin found Dad's skis in the basement, but his own were missing. And anyway, wouldn't they probably be too small for him? They decided to go buy new boots and skis for Benjamin. They walked across the parking lot, taking the gravel paths through the snow that led to the shopping center, and just when they got to the dry fountain, where homeless people often argued with each other in the summer, Dad suddenly brought his hand to his head. He staggered forward, reeling in a circle until he was back where he'd started. Benjamin grabbed on to him.

"What's going on?" he asked.

"Nothing," Dad said. "All of a sudden I just got such a headache." Dad stood there for a moment, his forehead creased, gazing down at the snow, and then he bent over to pick up his hat, which he'd dropped. That's when he fell over. Benjamin threw himself down over him, turned him onto his side, tried to get control of his flailing head. "I don't know what's happening," he whispered. "It's like something burst inside my head."

That's how it went, the morning Dad had his stroke.

———

THE AMBULANCE CAME, and the paramedics' detachment made Benjamin feel calm; they wouldn't have worked so slowly on someone who might be dying. They got out of their vehicles, examined Dad, and casually opened the back doors and pulled out the shiny metal stretcher. They let him lie down on it himself, fastened him in with a belt over his belly. Dad observed everything going on around him wide-eyed. One of the paramedics laid a gentle hand on Dad's arm, finally got his attention, and Dad looked him straight in the eye.

"You've had a stroke," said the man.

"You don't say?" Dad said. As if it were some amusing factoid.

No one was allowed to ride in the ambulance. Benjamin stood to the side and watched as they loaded Dad in. Their eyes met. Dad took Benjamin's hand, waved it like a flag. "And here we were supposed to go skiing," he said.

The door closed and the ambulance slowly maneuvered past the curious onlookers on the square.

Later on, Pierre and Benjamin and Mom gathered around Dad's bed in the ICU, and when the doctor arrived, the news was clear: everything had turned out okay after all. Dad had had a minor bleed in his brain, and the scan showed that none of his brain functions had been damaged. His oxygen levels were still low, and that was of mild concern to the doctor; Dad would be placed under observation in the hospital for a few days, but if all went well he would soon be able to come home again.

Nils, who lived outside the city, arrived at the hospital an hour later. With him was a woman in a wig. Benjamin knew who she was—they'd met once before, about six months ago, when Nils brought her for a Sunday dinner at Mom and Dad's. "You might be wondering about the wig," she said, just a few minutes into dinner. They were. The wig was blond, almost white, and had such a pronounced set of bangs that there could be no doubt it wasn't her real hair. The woman told them that this was the point. She had an illness that made her lose her hair. In a world where most people would be ashamed of being bald, she had decided to be the opposite. She didn't feel an ounce of shame, she said. She made the wig, the hair loss, all of it, into part of her identity. She talked fast and refused to be interrupted, and Benjamin was afraid that Mom would soon lose patience with her. She stroked Nils's arms on the table as she spoke, scratching him gently with her long nails. When Nils went to fill the water carafe, Benjamin watched him wandering toward the kitchen, saw that he was standing up straight, full of a confidence Benjamin didn't recognize.

Near the end of the meal, the woman with the wig took it off and placed it on the table beside her. She did it without comment, so no one else commented either, but an uncomfortable silence settled over the table like a lid, the clatter of flatware on china and all eyes sneaking looks at her smooth head, the light of the candles on the table gleaming against her skull. There she sat, the woman with a wig, now wigless, in the family's inner sanctum, behind every vault, like a lack of boundaries become flesh. Maybe she wanted to stir things up or make an impression, and maybe she succeeded for a little while, but once she'd left it was like stirring syrup: after a moment, everything was just as it had been.

The woman with the wig came to the hospital hand in hand with Nils, and she hugged each and every member of the family.

This was the first time Benjamin had seen Nils in months, but maybe it was thanks to her that their reunion felt simpler than Benjamin could have imagined. Dad was shaken. He peered at the rolling cart next to his bed with that searching gaze, like after dinner during summers at the cottage, when he was picking everyone else's plates clean. He looked at his children.

"The ambulance was scary," Dad said.

"I can imagine," said Benjamin.

Pierre handed him a glass of juice and Dad sucked thoughtfully at his straw as he gazed at the ceiling.

"But those ambulance guys were nice," Dad said.

"What did you talk about?" Pierre asked.

"They mostly asked a bunch of questions and made me do a bunch of silly things, to see how I was feeling."

"What kinds of things?"

"They asked if I could smile. And of course I could. Then they asked me to stretch out my hand and hold it there for five seconds. And then they asked me to repeat a simple sentence, to see if I was slurring."

"What was the sentence?" Benjamin asked.

Dad answered, but Benjamin couldn't understand what he said. A brief exchange of glances between the three sons.

After a while, Dad was tired and wanted to rest, and once he was asleep the family left the hospital; Mom said she would come back the next day. But Benjamin stayed, keeping watch over his sleeping father.

THE DAY PROGRESSED and it got dark early, the room grew dim, there was a stripe of warm yellow at the bottom of the door that led to the corridor, with black shadows moving across it each time someone passed. Dad woke up later, managed to sit up in bed and ask for strawberry juice. The evening went on, they sat there together, and a quiet rain fell outside. Perhaps that last conversation could have been put to better use. There were, of course, things that Benjamin wished he had said, afterward, or questions he wished he'd asked. Memories he needed help sorting, things he'd heard Dad say or do a long time ago that he still didn't understand. But they didn't talk about the past, they never had and they didn't now, because neither of them knew how to do it, and maybe it wasn't necessary, maybe this silence was the most beautiful thing they could have together, because it was just Benjamin and Dad, Mom wasn't there and they were free and clear, beyond her force field, like two prisoners who managed to break out and were recovering after their escape, savoring the silence together. They didn't talk, not really, but maybe they were still happy that day, as they looked around the room alertly, and sometimes their eyes met and they smiled at each other.

"This is all so silly," said Dad.

"What is?"

He lifted his hands, gestured at the room. "This."

"Yes, it is," said Benjamin.

"For us two, too," said Dad. He gazed at Benjamin with his watery eyes. "We were supposed to go out hunting."

Dad said he was tired and lay down on his side, and an hour into his sleep, he had his second stroke. Its only signs were a sharp intake of breath, a wrinkle between his eyebrows, and that the machines started beeping and the room was suddenly full of activity, and Benjamin stood pressed against the wall during all the feverish commotion, and then a doctor took him into the hall and told him that Dad wasn't going to pull through this time. Benjamin called the others, and they returned to the sickbed one by one. Pierre was last; he stormed in and was astonished to find that no one was fighting for Dad's life.

"Isn't there a doctor here?" Pierre asked.

"No," said Mom. "There's nothing they can do."

Someone had tilted Dad's bed in all the ruckus, so he was lying uphill, his head all the way up at the edge of the bed.

"Why is he lying like that?"

"It's . . ." Mom stopped, made a gesture with one hand, as if that would explain it.

Nils and the woman with the wig stood in the shadows, in the back of the room, leaning against the wall. The woman's wig was like a source of faint light. She was wearing a flimsy blouse tucked into a skirt, and her nipples were visible through the fabric. Also in the room was a nurse, sitting in a chair next to a machine that seemed to be monitoring Dad's pulse.

Benjamin had crawled up onto the edge of the bed, next to Dad, and placed a hand on his head. Dad was transformed: he suddenly looked thinner, his cheeks sunken, and his eyebrows wrinkled in concern as if he were having a bad dream. Benjamin shook his shoulder gently and whispered. "Dad. I'm here."

He rested his head on Dad's chest, to hear his heart beating; he closed his eyes and saw the cottage, the little path down to the lake. Dad is standing by the boathouse and untangling the nets; four perch have made a mess of them. Benjamin helps Dad by holding on to a loop of the mesh, lifting the bucket when a perch tumbles out, and the sun is shining between the birches, making a dappled pattern on Dad's white T-shirt, and Dad is focused on his task and suddenly he looks up and notices Benjamin, as if he'd forgotten he was there. They exchange smiles. "It's so nice of you to help me," says Dad. It's just Benjamin and Dad. And the wind rustling the birches.

Down by the lake one hot afternoon. Dad and Benjamin have set out towels next to each other on the shore. They've just taken a dip and they're lying on their backs in the sun. Dad asks if he can put his hand on Benjamin's shoulder. Benjamin wonders why, and Dad replies, "It's so reassuring to know you're still here." Then Dad's hand is resting on him, pressing him gently to the earth, and he closes his eyes, all his worry gone.

He's walking close behind Dad along the water's edge, on their way to the sauna. Dad calls out to Pierre and Nils: Do you want to sauna with us? No one is interested, and a tiny spark, a tiny point in Benjamin's chest catches fire—it's just him and Dad for a while. They go into the sauna. "You take the seat by the window," says Dad. "I want you to have the view of the lake." Dad says you have to listen carefully when you ladle water onto the heater, because you can hear the stones whispering, and Dad holds a finger up in the air and it hisses and spits as the water turns to steam and Dad whispers words of encouragement to the stones: "Take care of each other." He says, "Promise me you'll go out if it gets too hot." They compare their hands, stretching their arms out, before the window with the lake in the background. "I am you," Dad says.

Benjamin lay on Dad's chest and tried to hear his father's heart beating, and each fresh thought began at the cottage, and for the first time in many years he felt the urge to go back; he wanted to walk down to the shore, drain the water from the boat, push it out, see Dad's hair blowing in the wind. He looked up at the heart monitor. Dad's pulse was thirty-five. Benjamin didn't understand. Can you have a pulse of thirty-five and still be alive? It dropped to thirty-four, then thirty-three. The nurse turned the machine away from the family so they wouldn't have to look at it. And a few seconds later she nodded and said, concisely, "Now."

Mom was quick to confirm. "Now Dad is dead," she said.

Benjamin looked up, saw Pierre standing in the middle of the room as if he had decided to walk up to Dad and then changed his mind, his hands in the pockets of his jeans, and in the low light it looked like he was smiling as he cried. Nils approached slowly. His girlfriend came up and sat on the other side of the bed; she took off her wig, placed it beside her, and kissed Dad on the forehead. A sharp flash illuminated the walls. Nils had taken out a small camera, was standing at the foot of the bed taking picture after picture, the room lighting up with each flash.

And Benjamin looked at his father, and it was then, on his deathbed, that he recalled what had happened just that very morning when his dad had promised him a ski trip, and with the memory he suddenly realized why he had such a deep love for his father in spite of everything. The chance to be alone with Dad. It was those moments that had sustained him through the years, that had always made him stay on the right side of life. The moments when a window opened and brought a chance for something that belonged solely to Benjamin and his father, and they made plans together, whispered in excitement about everything they would do, as the moment of escape approached.

Soon it will happen.

Soon it will just be us, me and my dad.

18

6:00 A.M.

He leaves downtown by way of its empty streets, traveling high above the city on the raised concrete highways, the only car in all the five lanes. This is a rental car he's not entirely used to yet; he mistakes indicators for windshield wipers, isn't familiar with the stick shift or the clutch. The sound it makes when he accelerates at a green light downtown reminds him of when Dad missed third gear and got first by accident, and the car leapt and gave a desperate moan and Mom shouted that she'd had enough. Soon he's in the countryside, meadows and pastures and electric fences gleaming gently in the dawning sunshine, small lakes full of tall reeds in the morning light, suddenly a bright yellow field of rapeseed comes and goes, whiffs of cow manure from the farms, and the red houses with white trim surrounded by grain fields carefully outlined and squared up by tractors. He drives for nearly an hour, following the directions of the GPS lady. Her apathetic voice that might contain something more, a cautious resistance: Are you really sure you want to do this? He drives through the small villages, past half-hearted flea market signs, knotty tree trunks on either side of the road, like an endless avenue leading to a manor house, paved roads leading to smaller paved roads, he drives fast and crests a hill and there, in the middle of the road, stands a red deer. As if it's been waiting for him. He brakes so hard the tires screech, and the car stops a few yards from the animal. The deer isn't afraid, doesn't flee into the forest with hooves scraping the asphalt. He stays put and gazes in at the driver's seat. The engine had turned itself off with the violent braking, and Benjamin turns it on again; the deer doesn't react to the sound, and even when Benjamin revs the engine he doesn't make any effort to move. It's a huge animal, six feet tall, maybe even bigger? Benjamin didn't know red deer could get so big. He stands there, his feet planted wide, quiet and tranquil, as if he is purposefully blocking his passage, guarding something beyond. That reddish-brown pelt. Those massive horns, like winter trees on his head. His eyes look so lovely in the low sun, with the dark, gray clouds peering over the treetops.

There's something about making eye contact with a large animal. Benjamin remembers driving with Dad and his brothers one winter night, the asphalt white with whirling snow, the road edged by forest on both sides, swollen birches side by side with snow-heavy firs. Suddenly a moose calf was standing in the road, frozen in the winter like a portrait. Dad was going too fast, didn't have time to brake. The moose hit the front of the car and flew back along the side and was gone, behind them. Dad stopped and headed out into the snow to see what had become of the animal. The children watched him go as they waited in the car. The hazard lights turned the forest yellow. He came back after a while; the animal had vanished. Everyone got out to search for it along the shoulder, and at last they found it. The calf had limped a few yards into the forest and now there he lay. Benjamin remembers his eyes. They were wet and shiny, as if he were crying with gentle certainty that it was all over. He didn't try to get up, just lay there looking at the four of them up on the road, and the quartet returned his gaze. Dad dug around in the trunk and came back with a tire iron. What was he going to do with that? He told the children to turn around, that they shouldn't watch. "Look up," said Dad. "Look at the stars." And they looked up, the steam rising from the brothers' mouths, and the night was clear and it was a long way to the next town, no glowing lights to cloud their view, and the stars were sending him signals as if the universe were trying to get his attention from all directions. And it was like everything up there came closer, space pressing against his cheek, and the Milky Way made the sounds of the universe expanding, you could hear it all the way down there, a protracted creaking like when you draw back a bowstring and the wood complains. And he, a boy who so often felt like he was on the sidelines, felt at this moment like he and his brothers were the center of everything, as Dad disappeared into the forest with his tire iron and they stayed behind with their faces turned to the creaking sky.

Dad leapt back up to the road, shouting, "Come on, kids!" He hurried to the car and tossed the tool into the trunk. Benjamin looked up at the spot where the moose calf had lain down to die, but there were no eyes flashing there any longer. Then, in the car, the boys sat quietly in back and Dad slapped his bloody hands twice against the steering wheel and cried, blubbering like a child, all the way home.

Benjamin steps out of the car and slowly approaches the red deer, who looks over at the forest and then back at Benjamin. He lets him come very close. Benjamin hesitantly places a hand on the deer's muzzle. The animal stays put, gazing into his eyes, breathing calmly, warm air streaming through Benjamin's fingers. The chilly summer-dawn air has been warmed up in his lungs. Benjamin remembers the time he almost drowned in icy water and lost consciousness and was woken by warm water rushing over his hands. It was so nice, he wanted more, wanted the water to keep warming him. Only later did he realize that he had been throwing up water that had ended up in his lungs, and that's why it was warm; his lungs had warmed it before they sent it back out.

The deer snorts into Benjamin's hand and walks off, just a few tentative steps across the asphalt at first, but when he reaches the ditch he begins to weave confidently between the trees. After a moment he turns and looks back. He gazes at Benjamin, then starts moving again. Benjamin watches him until he's gone. He gets back in the car and keeps driving, and the GPS lady, who had followed the drama breathlessly and silently, resumes her gentle guidance, and after some time she grows more forceful, right, then left, then right again, and soon Benjamin has reached the home of his older brother. Benjamin looks up at the house, which is surrounded by a white picket fence. He honks twice, thinks he might see movement in the window closest to the door. Nils has lived here for several years, but this is the first time Benjamin has visited. It's smaller than he'd expected, a one-story brick house with a small yard in front. A lone apple tree in the yard. Nils comes out after a moment, with a bag over his shoulder and a sack Benjamin recognizes from yesterday—the boxes of frozen single-serving pierogi they found in Mom's freezer. There's a bowl in his hand, too. He stands on the steps to the small porch and gives a sharp whistle, and it doesn't take long before the cat comes slinking along the wall. Nils kneels down and sets the bowl on the ground. The cat circles it, noses it once, and walks off. She's gotten so fat. Benjamin remembers when the brothers bought her, at a cat rescue outside the city. It was love at first sight. They tried to determine what color she was, and the lady who ran the rescue, a chapped and red and inflamed sort of woman, said that the name of the color was "coffee with too much milk," and that description was so spot-on it made Benjamin laugh. Nils wanders down to the car, stuffs his luggage in the trunk and the bulging sack of food in the back seat, and then he climbs in next to Benjamin.

"Well, at least we've got plenty of food," Benjamin says.

Nils shoots him a quick glance, as if to gauge his mood, and Benjamin smiles and Nils laughs and runs his hand through his hair.

"The thing about pierogi is, if you eat one you'll want another," he says.

Benjamin looks up at the house, sees the cat approaching the bowl of food again.

"Everything good?" Nils asks.

"Yeah," says Benjamin. "I saw a red deer."

"A red deer?"

"Yeah. He was standing in the middle of the road and I had to slam on the brakes—the car stopped just a few yards away."

"Whoa," says Nils.

"Yeah, it could have been bad."

Silence between the brothers, a faint hum from the air-conditioning. Benjamin has both hands on the wheel, glances out at the treetops and sees a wall of dark clouds coming over the otherwise clear sky. He pulls into Nils's driveway and turns the car around, steering slowly back the way he came.

"If possible, turn around," says the GPS lady.

But it's too late for that. There's no getting out of this now, no stopping what's been set in motion. He shoots a look at his brother.

"Let's do this," he says.

"Let's do this," Nils responds.

And they drive through the early morning, past the sleeping houses, and when they get out on the open roads that cut between fields Benjamin discovers that they're driving straight toward the storm. It's low in the sky, as if the rain has weighted the clouds. The sun is still shining on the car, but there's no mistaking it: it's chaos in the city. Benjamin looks at the clock. He's had nothing to do his whole life, but suddenly everything is happening all at once, so many things have to fit into this day and there's so little time. Just on the other side of a crest Benjamin sees two skid marks on the asphalt; he slows down, orients himself, and cries, "Here it is!" Nils, whose eyes have been on his phone, looks up. Benjamin backs the car up until the skid marks are in front of them.

"This was where I braked! For the deer."

"Oh, shit," says Nils. He leans forward to see. "You really had to brake hard."

Benjamin looks at the parallel black lines on the road. Looks at the forest. He brings his hand to his nose, sniffs his fingertips—there's still a faint whiff of the deer on them. And then he keeps driving.

"It happened," Benjamin mumbles.

"What did you say?" Nils asks.

"Oh, nothing."

But it is something. Because the instant the red deer disappeared into the forest, Benjamin began to wonder if it had really happened, or if he had imagined the whole thing. He didn't know, couldn't tell, and just now when he heard himself telling Nils about it, he didn't quite believe himself, didn't think it sounded believable. And by the time they left Nils's house he was convinced: he'd made it all up. It was as if reality wanted to give him a sign by way of the tracks on the asphalt. It happened. There in the car with his brother by his side, with the sun at his back and the storm far ahead, in a silence he doesn't have to wrestle with, he feels free of anxiety for the first time in a long time. "I'm glad we're doing this," Benjamin says.

"Me too," says Nils.

He turns on the car radio; it's a song he recognizes and he gently drums the rhythm against the wheel. They're getting closer to the big city, driving high above it on the concrete overpasses, still completely alone, as if the five-lane roads were built just for them, to make sure they would have free passage on this important journey, and in the city the café owners are opening their security grilles and removing the locking cables from the outdoor seating, and the brothers park outside Pierre's door and wait for a while. Eventually Nils has to call, and soon he comes down with a small suitcase and a garment bag, which he tosses into the trunk.

"There's a real turd-floater coming," he says, glancing at the clouds as he gets into the car.

"Well put," says Nils. "Truly."

"Thanks," says Pierre.

Benjamin laughs.

He pulls out, navigating cautiously past the double-parked cars. Pierre fiddles with his phone, asks Benjamin to link it to the stereo system, and he puts on a song Benjamin recognizes right away.

"Thought it would be a good soundtrack for our trip," Pierre says with a grin. It's Lou Reed, and Benjamin smiles when he thinks about everything they're about to do, all the enormous weight that lies ahead of them, and how the brothers sync up by way of the music, sheltered by the irony.

When the chorus comes they fill their lungs with air, Pierre shouts "Turn it up" and rolls down the window, and all three of them sing, through smiling lips, "Oh, it's such a perfect day, I'm glad I spent it with you." Pierre puts both hands in the air and makes V signs, Nils is less demonstrative, of course, but Benjamin glances at him, sees he's singing at the top of his voice.

He looks at his brothers, thinks he loves them.

They head south through the city, toward the cemetery, three brothers on their way to pick up the remains of their mother, and the song echoes through the crappy speakers and across the fateful morning. The light turns red suddenly and Benjamin slams on the brakes.

"Hey!" Pierre shouts. "Take it easy."

"We don't want another incident," Nils says.

Pierre looks up from his phone. "What?" he says. "What do you mean, another incident?"

"Benjamin almost hit a red deer earlier."

"Shit," says Pierre.

"It was a close one," Benjamin says.

Benjamin thinks of the deer, their remarkable moment there on the country road. How the deer turned around partway into the forest, as if he were waiting for him there, wanted him to come along. "Remember the moose calf when we were little?" Benjamin asks.

"What?" Nils says.

"The time Dad hit a moose," Benjamin says. "And we went to look for it and found it in the forest. And Dad beat it to death with a tire iron."

The song is over; the car falls silent. Pierre looks out the window.

Nils turns to Benjamin.

"Dad hit a moose?" Nils asks.

"What are you talking about, don't you remember? Dad made us stand by the road and look up at the stars, because he didn't want us to see. And then he cried the entire way home."

Nils looks down at his phone, bringing up window after window, browsing through menus. Benjamin stares at them in surprise, first at Nils, then through the rearview mirror at Pierre, who clears his throat and averts his eyes, looking at the road.

"Don't you remember?"

They don't respond.

A car honks behind them. The light is green. Benjamin shifts into first and drives, the world grows dark, he squints to see the road. The sky opens up and an insane downpour engulfs the car, and soon after the rain comes the wind. Benjamin can see the signs of it in the sudden darkness, in the pennants tugging at their poles above hotel façades, and in a pedestrian leaning into the storm as he walks down the sidewalk. This is the sort of wind that might blow a city away, a storm that should have a human name.

19

THE BIRTHDAY PRESENT

Mom lived on the busiest street downtown. Four lanes, a major route plowing through the high-rises, trucks stopped at the traffic light outside Mom's window and the air brakes hissed. Diesel buses lined up at the stop, the draft from the subway entrance knocked at the trash bins. The escalator, always out of order, its status reported, according to the red note that was taped over the black rubber. Thousands of pieces of gum on the concrete slabs. The illegal cabs came one after the next, rattling off destination suggestions in broken Swedish. The sidewalk cafés all in a line, their awnings in constant turbulence from the wind kicked up by traffic. Benjamin waited for the Walk sign, looked up at Mom's two windows on the second floor. He could see black helium balloons on the ceiling in there, their strings hanging in the air. Perhaps a glimpse of her in the kitchen window; a figure bending over the sink, maybe that was her. She looked like a stranger, someone who was pretending to live there, simulating kitchen chores.

Dad hated downtown and would run errands there only to pick something up from the market halls, and he always came back upset and in a bad mood. The fact that Mom had moved here felt like a protest against him, or at least a dispute with the life she had lived with him. Just a week after the funeral, Mom had put the apartment up for sale and informed her two youngest sons that this might be a good time for them to find their own places to live. She wanted to move as soon as possible, as if to demonstrate that she had always been a prisoner of Dad's choices, and now that she was free she could finally live the life she wanted. The old family furniture had been discarded or put in storage; it wouldn't fit in her one-bedroom apartment. Dad's library was gone, that whole inviting wall of books in his bedroom that he had spent so much time puttering with when he was alive. The first time Benjamin visited Mom's new apartment he walked around in silence. He couldn't look at what was left in the apartment, could only think of everything that wasn't from the last one.

Benjamin pressed the intercom button even though he knew how much it annoyed Mom that he hadn't memorized the door code. After a moment it crackled to life and the door unlocked. He walked into the cold lighting, heading for the elevator. Mom had lived in the apartment for three years now, and sometimes she invited Benjamin over for a meal, the dinner full of polite tension, quiet conversation between bites and silence through clinking flatware, and by coffee time Mom had turned inward, taken out the newspaper and a pencil. She smoked cigarettes and made notes in the margins of the travel section, muttering destinations aloud: "Lanzarote, no. Tenerife, no. Sharm el-Sheikh . . . Morocco . . . never been there. Could be fun." And then she made up her mind, left just a few days later, bought a single airline ticket, always alone, came back a week later, and Benjamin might tentatively inquire about what she'd done on these trips, and Mom would say, "No idea." She lay in the sunshine, she said, and if she was lucky she met someone nice to talk to, but sometimes she was just alone. One time she came back and told him that she hadn't spoken to a single person the whole trip. Benjamin would have thought this was an embarrassing thing to admit, a sign of failure or loneliness, but her dignity seemed intact. Almost cheerful, wound up by the realization: She hadn't used her mouth to speak in seven days! And then she sat there with the newspaper again, tanned, looking for more trips to take. Benjamin always thought it was so pointed and strange that she never asked if he wanted to come on any of these trips, but she seemed to take it for granted—it was a given that she would always go alone. Their brief encounters, full of silence. Each time he visited Mom's, he hurried home again to use the bathroom, his stomach always uneasy. He would sit on the toilet for a long time, in silence, letting the stomach cramps come.

It was like they were always on their guard with each other, except for when they were drinking. Maybe that was the only time, those evenings when they went to one of the sidewalk cafés down on the street and had a beer together, that they could relax in each other's company. They would have an appetizer and drink until they were drunk. When the restaurant closed they would weave across the street and sit down at the pub. There they drank harder, with greater focus. They sat among the young people, students who were drawn in by the cheap beer and lax ID enforcement. Loud music, and Mom's eyes watery and her voice raspier, she got drastic and a little careless, firing off racial slurs, aware of the lazy amusement of it. And Benjamin followed her, he could play this role too, they had their most relaxed conversations in the bar, exchanging witty but empty words and gossip, and drank and drank until they grew thick skin and stopped feeling the cold draft from the door. At no point, not even when she was drunk, did Mom touch upon her grief, and she never asked about Benjamin's. Except for one single time, on one of those nights when they drank particularly hard and didn't get home until two in the morning—Benjamin was sitting on the toilet, emptying his anxious belly, when he got a text from Mom.

"I'm not sure I want to be here anymore," she wrote.

"Be where?" Benjamin asked.

She didn't reply, and afterward Benjamin lay in bed trying to understand, seeing images of what that might entail.

Now Benjamin rang the doorbell, heard the click of heels on the floor, which stopped as she reached the welcome mat and the door opened.

"Hi, sweetie," said Mom, and they hugged. He smelled Mom's air freshener, which she'd sprayed throughout the apartment to get rid of the smoke smell. The scent of tropical fruit and cigarettes. The lights were out in the apartment, lit candles everywhere. He hung up his coat and peered in. A few other guests. A late-middle-aged woman dripping with jewelry, heavy earrings that pulled her earlobes toward the floor, an old work friend of Mom's, as far as Benjamin knew. And a woman in stocking feet, dressed in black, the neighbor from the third floor, she explained. In a row on the sofa sat a group of people who didn't resemble one another but clearly belonged together. Benjamin introduced himself, and they told him they were members of Mom's salsa-dancing group. They eyed him with interest, smiling, responsive to him, watching him, and Benjamin took some pleasure in that, maybe because they knew who he was—Mom had told them about him. She'd said very little about her dancing. Benjamin recalled that she'd received a flyer in the mail last Christmas about a salsa group that was looking for new members. She had gone to check it out, but Benjamin hadn't known she'd kept going. Mom sat down on the sofa, refilled her salsa friends' wineglasses. Benjamin spotted Pierre by the window and went to stand beside him.

"People aren't exactly pouring in," Pierre whispered.

"It's an open house," Benjamin said. "We have no idea how many people have already been here."

"True. And the gift table is practically groaning." Benjamin looked over at the three presents. He laughed.

"How did it go with our present?" Benjamin asked.

"Everything's on track—Nils will be here with it any second."

Mom had made canapés with salmon and soft cheese; they were on a platter on the dining table, along with seafood salad croustades. A few bottles of bubbly on a tray along with champagne glasses. Benjamin took in the room. Only now, with strangers inside it, could Benjamin see the apartment as an outsider. The Jewish authors in the small bookcase. A photograph of a Nobel laureate author on the wall. An attempt at academic respectability, one Benjamin recognized from his childhood. The brothers had received an upper-class upbringing that had somehow occurred below the poverty line. Raised like nobility, taught always to hold their heads high, always to say grace before a meal and shake hands with Mom and Dad before leaving the table. But there had been no money, or: very little of the money had been invested in the children. And the academic upbringing had been undertaken halfheartedly; it began with great to-do but was never completed. The children were never as well educated as their parents, and that gave rise to funny stories, recurring anecdotes about how the children didn't understand the wonders that surrounded them. Mom's favorite: the times she'd prepared crudités, a French appetizer that consisted of vegetables with dipping sauces, and the children thought she had made "cruddy tea." This was in the early years, when the kids were quite small, and when Mom and Dad still had energy and pep. When the project that was their family still had momentum. But later on most of that vanished. Things stopped working. The frequency of their dinners gradually slowed, without anyone noticing, and once they stopped completely no one really thought about it. Each evening at six the children wandered into the kitchen and made themselves sandwiches and ate them silently with chocolate milk. The only thing that survived was Sunday dinners, when Mom made an effort, standing in the kitchen dripping soy sauce into the cream sauce until it reached the right shade. Dinners with lots of wine, but most of the time the only noticeable difference was that Mom and Dad grew ponderous and quiet, turned inward. Sometimes when they were done eating, Mom would suddenly roar. "Excuse me!" she'd shout as the brothers set their drinking glasses on their empty plates and stood up from the din-

ner table. "Do we leave the table without thanking the cook?"
And the confused children had to walk up to her, one after the
next, shake her hand and bow, like a relic of a time they hardly
remembered.

A middle-aged woman extricated herself from the sofa and
clinked two champagne glasses together. She said that while
she certainly couldn't speak for the salsa group in an official
capacity, she was speaking for all of them when she said she
truly enjoyed Mom's presence on Thursdays. They weren't a
big group, nor were they world champions of Latin dance—but
they appreciated one another's company, and during the past
year they'd become quite a tight gang. They were so glad for the
chance to come over to Mom's and celebrate her fiftieth birthday, and they had a small gift from the group, she said as she
fumbled for the bag she'd placed at the foot of the sofa. Because
now you're a real *salserita,* she said, emphasizing each vowel, and
this is from all of us, including Larsa and Yamel, who, sadly,
couldn't be here to celebrate with us. The woman handed over
a small package and Mom's eyes sparkled as she said "Oh, my"
and tore open the paper to reveal a glittery black skirt, which
she immediately held up to her waist.

"I've had my eye on something like this for so long," Mom
cried, doing a little pirouette to show it off to the room.

"And you know what this means, don't you?" said the
woman. "We want to see a little dance, don't we?"

Immediate chattering enthusiasm, loud protests from Mom,
cries and hoots from the sofa, and after a moment she gave
in, disappeared into the bedroom to change. Amid murmurs
from the sofa, Pierre turned to the window, digging through
his pockets for his cigarettes. Benjamin gazed at the faces of the

expectant dance friends, those strange people who had grown so close to Mom, and he thought maybe he had been wrong. He'd thought Mom had stopped living, but maybe she'd just stopped living with him, with her family.

Cheers erupted as Mom came out in her new skirt, which had a low waist and a high slit. A small gap of skin between the skirt and her tight blouse, the white band of her belly. Benjamin saw the marks on her abdomen, the scars from her c-sections. He remembered when he was little, lying on the sofa or the bed with Mom, and she would show him the little notches just below her belly button. "That one's Nils," she said, pointing at one scar. "And there's Pierre. And that small one, that's you."

Benjamin gently touched the little pockets on Mom's belly with the tip of his finger, felt her warm skin.

Mom went over to the stereo in the bookcase, switched one CD for another, the living room perfectly silent now. The music started, and Benjamin had the sense that a few too many instruments were playing at once, like a web of different rhythms trying to settle into one another. Mom went to the big area rug in the middle of the living room, stopped at the dining table, drank from a glass of wine, and took up her starting position: both hands over her head, as if she were adjusting a bun. And then she performed the first steps to a few happy cries from her friends on the sofa. She fell into character, became a different person. She lifted her knees, stepping back and forth, her hands stretched down along her sides, and then she began to gyrate, her upper body still and her waist moving as if she were on a horse, a movement that intensified as she turned, and it took him a moment to notice it in the dim lighting, but her eyes were closed. At first he thought she was dancing as if for a large audience, that she was imagining a dance floor bathed in spotlights from all directions, a black sea of onlookers surrounding her, but he soon realized it was the other way around. She was dancing as if no one else were in the room, like when she was a little girl, in her childhood bedroom, on the bed, making these motions for herself, in her absolute solitude, and that was why she was so free in this moment, because nothing had happened yet. Mom opened her eyes, looked at Benjamin and put a hand out toward him, and she pulled him onto the dance floor. He was struck by embarrassment, tried to resist, but Mom was determined. Her bent knees, her white thighs flashing from underneath the skirt. She closed her eyes, dancing alone again, within herself, and Benjamin stopped moving in rhythm, stood right in front of his mother and watched her move, dreamlike, and suddenly Mom looked up at him, grabbed his hand, and pulled him into her arms. He hadn't been so close to her for many years, not since he was a child. To feel her embrace, that there was a thin thread between them that hadn't broken, a longing for her that had never faded. He smelled her scent, felt her breath at his ear. There he stood, beside his mother again. He didn't want to let go.

Decisively, firmly, Mom pushed him away and retreated back into herself. The song ended and the room applauded, Mom gesturing at Benjamin as if to recognize his contribution as well. She sat down on the sofa, drained, happy, allowed someone to hand her a glass.

Pierre showed him a text, from Nils: "Outside." Benjamin and Pierre went out. There he was, at the door, in his big down jacket, with a small kitten in his arms.

"Did you bring the bow?" Nils asked.

Pierre pulled a pink silk ribbon from his back pocket, and the kitten put up a fight, its legs went stiff and it showed its claws, as Pierre tied it up like a package. The brothers had gotten together the week before, at a cat rescue outside the city, and wandered from cage to cage until they fell for this cream-colored little animal. When Benjamin saw the kitten in Nils's arms there in the hall, it looked smaller than he remembered, so small that it couldn't be real, because surely such tiny cats didn't exist. Pierre tied the bow. "Wait here, I'm going to say a few words," Pierre said to Nils.

Benjamin and Pierre went inside, stood at the entrance to the living room. Pierre cleared his throat, and when no one heard him he tried again, louder, coughing noisily and clearing his sinuses. The conversation on the sofa stopped and all eyes turned to Pierre.

"What do you give the woman who has everything?" he cried. "My brothers and I have been giving a lot of thought to that question, leading up to this day. After all, we know she doesn't want any goddamn *things*!"

Someone on the sofa chuckled. Mom's back was ramrod straight; she was on alert.

"So we thought, Forget that. We won't give her any things. We'll give her something of actual value."

He called out to Nils, who emerged from the dark hallway and entered the living room with the kitten in his arms. A murmur from the sofa, but Mom didn't understand, didn't know what she was looking at. Nils went up to Mom and handed her the animal, placing it gently in her lap.

"So cute I could just die!" said one of the guests.

Mom looked at the kitten. She laughed, then uttered a shrill sound. "You're all nuts!" she cried. "Is this for me?"

The brothers nodded.

"At first we wanted to get you a dog," said Pierre. "But then we thought a cat might be easier, in the city. And then we found her, and we just felt like . . ." He went over to the cat and held a finger to her nose. "We felt like she was yours."

"Oh my God," Mom mumbled, letting her hand rest gently on the kitten's head. She placed it on her bare belly. "She's wonderful."

It seemed to have gone well. That wasn't always the case. Mom was often annoyed when she had a birthday, didn't want any attention. She didn't feel particularly loved, she said, and didn't want people to put on an act once a year. But the family tried, with Dad the driving force but always clumsy in his attempts to make Mom happy. One time Dad gave Mom a quit-smoking course, and she was so insulted that she put an end to the festivities and went to bed. Benjamin remembers the time Dad helped him buy a toiletry case for Mom, and when she opened it she immediately suspected that it wasn't Benjamin, but Dad, who had paid for it, and she confronted Benjamin. But this seemed to have worked. Mom was entranced, her head bent toward the cat, stroking her fur gently.

"And we were thinking . . ." Pierre paused for effect. "We were thinking her name could be Molly."

Benjamin shot Pierre a look. Pierre was nodding in satisfaction, looking at Mom. He didn't mean anything by it. It was just a short circuit, Benjamin knew that, something he said in the moment, because he felt like the present was a success and that success could be prolonged, that the hole in his chest could be filled up faster with even more of Mom's love, that he was about to reach even deeper into Mom's heart.

He didn't mean to.

Mom looked up from the cat. "What did you just say?" she asked.

"As an homage," said Pierre, his voice now tinged with uncertainty.

"We never agreed on that," Benjamin said sharply. He turned to Pierre, lowered his voice: "What are you talking about?"

"You know what?" Mom said, looking at the brothers. She stopped herself, began to cry, someone in her dance group laid a hand on her bowed back. As she looked up again, Benjamin saw the pendulum moving, sorrow turning to rage. "You can leave now," she said.

Mom stood up, placed the kitten on the sofa, and left the living room.

It was so quiet that Benjamin could hear Mom in the kitchen, hear her sobs, could even make out the scratch of the match as she lit a cigarette. He stayed put, in front of the furniture, his eyes on the floor. And then it just happened. It wasn't as if he made a decision, it just happened. Quick as a wink everything went black, like in a movie when the diamond thief fumbles and the alarm goes off and iron grilles clatter down to block every exit. Benjamin felt his heart beat faster, the gates fell, one by one, and in the darkness he identified a feeling about his mother he had never in his life allowed to come out. Wrath. A tiny spark was all it took, one spark to ignite everything.

He went to the kitchen and stood in the doorway.

Mom was on a chair at the kitchen table. There were streaks of black under her eyes, smeared makeup.

"You can't forget Molly, but you forgot us a long time ago."

She looked at Benjamin in bafflement. He had never raised his voice to her before. He felt tears burning in his eyes, cursed himself, he didn't want to start blubbering. He didn't want to be sad, he wanted to be angry.

"We are here!" he shouted. "Me and Nils and Pierre. We are here."

Mom didn't say anything. And then came the sharp gasp and the tears, despite it all. He buried his face in his hands and headed for the door. He walked through the silence of the living room and left.

Out on the street he found himself standing outside the building door. For a moment he thought he would wait for his brothers there, that they would probably come down soon. He waited a few minutes, then left, walked past the sidewalk cafés and through the crosswalk. On the other side of the street he looked up at Mom's apartment but didn't see anyone in the windows, just the helium balloons on the ceiling like sad eyes gazing down at the living room in distress. He looked at the door. Where are my brothers, he thought.

He kept walking, alongside the insane traffic, plastic bags cavorting at the edge of the sidewalk, trash heading north, even the garbage wanted to get out of there. He walked toward the subway entrance. He turned around once more, gazing back at the building.

Where are my brothers?

20

4 : 0 0   A . M .

The room is closing in.

He shuts his eyes and maybe he sleeps, he thinks so, because when he opens his eyes again the room is brighter. He looks at the window, he can see a scrap of sunlight on the very top of the building across the street. A tiny yellow corner of the gray concrete. He has seen more sunrises than sunsets in his life. All the early summer mornings spent lying in his bed and watching the dawn creep out of the darkness outside his window like a nightmare, first gray and then milky and then the first rays of sun appeared on the treetops. He would approach the window to look at it, amazed, because it was a strange thing to see at first, a backward experience—the sun was in the wrong spot, shining from the wrong direction and at odd angles. But these days the sunrise is associated with so many other things—it's been fourteen days since Mom died and he still hasn't slept through the dawn. When the therapist asked Benjamin how he felt after Mom's death, he responded that he didn't feel anything, but maybe that wasn't true, maybe he felt so many things that it was impossible to distinguish a single emotion. He had to tell her his whole story, and she told him the brain is a remarkable organ. It does things we're not aware of. Sometimes, when you experience trauma, your mind will alter your memories. Benjamin had asked why, and the therapist replied: So you can bear it.

She said: Force yourself to think about your mother. And he countered with a question: What should I think about? Anything, the therapist said.

His first memory of his mother. He is three years old. Mom and Dad are in bed one morning, and they call for him: "Come here and give us a kiss!" He crawls up, getting tangled in the sheets as he goes. He kisses Dad, can hardly reach his lips for all the beard. He kisses Mom. And then he wipes his mouth, a quick stroke. He is confronted. Mom and Dad saw what he did. Mom lifts him to her, says, "Do you think it's gross to kiss us?"

His last memory of his mother. Her grimace as she died at the hospital. The expression her face got stuck in, that wolf-like grin. He has carried it with him ever since Mom's death, and every time it pops up in his mind he is thrown back to his childhood because it reminds him of something he once saw. He used to lick his fingertips when the skin there got dry. Mom told him to stop and began to imitate him when he couldn't quit. Each time he licked his fingers, she ran over and stuck her hands in her mouth and showed her teeth in a sneer. Benjamin searched her eyes for a hint of mischief, something to suggest that she was teasing him with love, but he never found it.

Fourteen days since she died. The doctors said death had come quickly, but it wasn't true. It took two weeks for her to die, from the time she felt the first stomach pains until it was over. But he supposed she'd received the death sentence one year earlier, when they discovered the tumor, the one she informed her sons of in a curt text and then refused to talk about. She never wanted company at the hospital and when they asked about treatment all she would say was that it was going well. She pretended she wasn't sick, and a few months later, when she claimed she had been given a clean bill of health, Benjamin didn't believe her, because he could tell that something was still wrong. She lost weight. Imperceptibly, seamlessly, deceptively, she lost pound after pound until one day Benjamin discovered that she was a different person. Her collarbones were sharp and angular, and the hollows beneath them formed dark pits. All the extra skin that folded around her. She became so frail and thin, susceptible to a breeze, that Benjamin had to hold her gnarled hands when they took walks. One time she mentioned that she had been to the doctor to discuss her weight. Her voice cheery, she told him that she now weighed eighty-eight pounds. "Can you believe it?" she said. "That's what a baby pig weighs!" Mom was given a few jars to take home, nutritional supplements in powder form, and they stood untouched on the counter for a few months before she threw them out.

The stomach pain came on suddenly. She was in a furniture store and it just exploded. The pain was so terrible, and she didn't know what it could be. She told her children that she had pressed her thumb into her waist and lay down with her belly over the arm of one of the display sofas, doing the strange tricks she'd learned as a child. The pain vanished but was soon back, and it only got worse. She stopped going out, she couldn't sleep at night, just lay awake in agony, and there were no painkillers that helped. Chasing sleep took over her life. She turned off the phone, because she wanted to sleep. It became harder to reach her, the phone turned off, brief texts in the middle of the night that seemed more and more confused. When Benjamin asked how she felt, she kept replying, "Tarzan." Then contact ceased entirely. Mom's phone was always off, and there were no signs of life. After three days of silence, Benjamin went over to her place, even though he knew she hated unannounced visits. He rang the doorbell a few times until at last she opened it, her hair standing on end. The windows were open, even though it was chilly out. The smell of detergent and vomit.

"Have you been sick?" he asked.

"Yes, I don't know why I'm throwing up so much," she replied.

She sank into her easy chair, took out a cigarette but immediately put it back. She hunched forward, her elbows on her knees. Her robe revealed scrawny legs, the skin hanging down on either side of her thighbones.

"Shouldn't we go to the hospital so they can take a look at you?" he asked.

"No, no," she said. "I'm fine. Just need to get some sleep."

He remembers how small she looked in the big chair. Mom leaned over and spat tentatively on the floor. This was a distinct signal for him—you only do that if you're awfully sick. She didn't protest, either, when he said they had to go to the emergency room right away, just stayed in the chair as he packed her a bag, and then they left. She was talkative on that first after-noon. She complained about her pain with what seemed like annoyance. Each time a nurse came into the room, she asked, "Do you know why I'm in so much pain?" Mumbled answers; they directed her to ask the doctor, who would be there soon.

He saw it all, remembers every detail. He remembers the room Mom was in. On the table next to her lay her dentures, a glass of apple juice, the evening papers, and a plate of lasagna she hadn't touched. She lay there with an IV in her arm and something that looked like a thimble on her index finger; it measured her oxygen levels. At regular intervals, a nurse came in to check her vital signs and make a note or two. He didn't dare to ask whether everything was okay.

He went home and returned the next morning. It was the last time they saw each other. Pierre and Nils were already there. They had given her morphine for the pain, and he sat at the edge of the bed and gazed into her confusion. She said she had had such strange dreams. She was in an airplane that was flying above a city, way too close to the rooftops, she tried to tell the flight attendants that they were too close, that it was danger-ous, but no one would listen.

It was Pierre's birthday, and he joked about it. "Are you going to give me my presents now, or do you want to wait?" he asked. Mom's confused look there in bed. She didn't know it was his birthday. But her confusion was greater than that, as if she couldn't quite grasp the concept of birthdays. She opened her mouth, then closed it thoughtfully.

"I'm kidding, Mom."

Nils had brought the morning editions, and he read the news aloud to her, but after a while she wanted him to stop.

She drank some juice, grimaced, screamed in pain, and held her stomach. And then she began to stare at the wall with her strangely deformed face. The brothers tried to reach her, but she didn't say a word, just stared doggedly at the wall. She met death silently. Wouldn't respond to questions; when you squeezed her hand she didn't squeeze back. The brothers watched quietly. And suddenly, without warning, her heart stopped beating and she was gone.

"The time is four twenty-five P.M.," said Nils, and that was so typical of him, to be the grieving son and the keeper of order all at the same time.

He has to sleep.

He can't face this day without getting some sleep. He won't make it through. He knows what he has to do. He has to talk with his brothers about things they haven't touched for twenty years. He flips his pillow over and lies on his other side. Catches sight of the framed photograph of the three brothers on the nightstand. It was taken at the water's edge down by the lake at the cottage. Benjamin, Pierre, and Nils, sun in their hair, wearing underpants and boots, tanned little-boy bodies. Bright colors, orange life jackets against a steel-gray sky. They're heading out to drop the net. Benjamin is in the middle, holding his brothers, one arm around each neck. Their bodies are relaxed, free. They're laughing at something unexpected. It's not that they're smiling for the picture, it's something else, as if Dad said something really funny right before he clicked the shutter, to catch them by surprise. They're laughing so hard they can barely breathe. They're holding each other. They're luminous, the brothers.

What happened to them?

Right after Mom died. They were together in her hospital room, and yet they were alone. Not once did they hold each other that afternoon. Nils brought out a camera and began to take pictures of Mom. Pierre went out on the little balcony across the hall and smoked a cigarette. Benjamin stood where he was, in the middle of the room. Then he left without saying good-bye. They couldn't help each other. It's been this way as long as he can remember, as long as he's been grown up. None of them really knows what to do, how to even look each other in the eye; their conversations take place with their gazes cast down at the tablecloth, quick spasms of communication. Sometimes he thinks about everything that's happened to them, how tightly they pressed to each other when they were little, and how odd everything is now: they treat each other like strangers. It's not just him, he thinks, it's all three of them. He's seen Nils pick up his cat as he comes to greet them, using her like a shield, an excuse not to hug them. One early morning, he suddenly saw Pierre coming toward him downtown. Pierre hadn't spotted Benjamin, because his eyes were on his phone, as always, blind to the world, living his life bathed in pale light from below, and Benjamin didn't say anything, didn't do anything, walked straight past him without announcing his presence. Their jackets brushed as they passed. He turned around and gazed after Pierre, saw the shape of his brother growing smaller and more diffuse, with a rising sorrow that bordered on panic. What happened to us?

What they're about to do seems unthinkable. This journey back to the cottage no one talks about anymore. His and Pierre's way of dealing with their childhood is to joke about it. He texts his brother that he'll be late and Pierre replies, "I'll pay for the taxi," imitating Dad's recurring, hysterical habit of trying to reel in his children when he was lonely for company. Pierre texts to say he wants to change the time they'll meet up and Benjamin replies, "Know what, let's just forget this whole project," a sarcastic reference to Mom's volatility. He has, however, never joked with Nils that way. Outside the window, the sun is slowly rising, the yellow spot on the concrete has expanded; now it covers almost the entire façade, burning over rows of blinds that shield bedrooms across the way. One window is open in the apartment, but he can't hear anything coming through it. The city is sleeping. He gets out of bed, makes a cup of coffee in the kitchen. He walks out onto the small balcony. A small table and a small chair and an ashtray full of cigarette butts. Hanging over the railing, a planter of forgotten tulips that are bent and yellowed in the dry soil. It's early, but it's already warm out. Clear sky, but to the east he can see a corner of the sea, and the sky above it is dark with clouds. It's close, like before a big storm. He looks at the clock. The gas station where he's going to pick up the rental car will open soon.

And then he sets out. Closing the door to the apartment for the last time, locking it. And soon he's sitting in the rental car. He leaves downtown by way of its empty streets, traveling high above the city on the raised concrete highways, the only car in all the five lanes.

21

THE GRAVEL ROAD

It was a couple of days after Mom died. He'd stayed at home since it happened, but now he was leaving for the first time. He walked through the city's largest park, the one that led down to the pier. He observed the treetops above his head. He knew it was the beginning of June and that the leaves were dark green, but it had been many years since his eyes could discern such a thing. After the accident at the substation he had been taken to the hospital. He had burns on his arms and the back of his neck and down his whole back; the doctors who would patch him up couldn't tell what was clothing and what was skin. After a few days at the hospital, before he was discharged, Dad asked the doctor if Benjamin would have any lasting issues. Impossible to say, he replied. He could very well have lifelong problems. Nerve damage that might not show up for years. His muscles might wither away slowly; there was a risk of heart arrhythmias, brain damage, kidney failure.

None of that happened. But the doctor didn't mention anything about sight. He didn't warn Benjamin that he might see colors differently after the explosion. There were some colors he couldn't see at all anymore. He couldn't see blue. He could lean down toward a thicket, get on all fours, and even if someone beside him insisted that it was full of blueberries, he couldn't see a single one. Other colors were brighter now—a few hours before the sun set in the spring and summer, he could see an arc of light rising above the horizon, the whole sky turning dark pink. It was so beautiful, it was a shame it wasn't real. When he was younger, he sometimes impressed one kid or another by staring straight into the sun without even blinking. His classmates would gather around him, shouting, drawing in others to come and look. Signal colors made him calm and he sought them out. He lingered near red traffic cones at road construction sites. Sometimes he went into sporting stores, to the fishing section, and rested his eyes on the lures, yellow and red, glowing like neon. But he remembers the trees of his youth, the weeks spent at the cottage in early June, leaves bursting with green energy. For a long time he missed being able to see them. Then he stopped caring.

He walked down to the water. The old fishing boats that had been renovated into housing for eccentrics. He kept going along the waterfront, passing the white passenger ferries docked along the quay. The restaurants advertising "catch of the day" and hoping to lure in the tourists who had no idea that nothing grew in this water, no fish lived here, because the sea was dead. The people around him were dressed for summer, but the weather had an April chill, flimsy collars turned up, goose bumps on bare arms. He had walked here a lot recently. Through the park to the pier and back up. He was taking walks more frequently; sometimes they were hours long. In the winter he might be so cold by the time he got back that he was numb; he would try to unlock the door but couldn't do it, and he stood there, fascinated, staring at his hand, how it couldn't hold the key, turn it in the lock. He often walked through the city without a destination in mind, through cemeteries and down into subway stations, riding to the next station and walking on. He had decided to put the accident behind him, but it didn't work out as he'd expected. His thoughts kept moving in that direction anyway. Each time he heard a loud noise, saw a bright light, any sort of disruption he wasn't prepared for, he was there again, in the transformer room. It still happened several times a day. Unexpected sudden sights cast him right back there. Or heat, when he opened the oven and bent down to see if the food was ready and the wave of hot air hit him. He would suddenly start sobbing. Sudden noises. Not just clear reports, like when teenagers were playing with firecrackers in the subway. The scrape of a chair when someone stood up in an empty restaurant. The sound of knives and forks being roughly sorted into a silverware drawer. He couldn't be in a bathroom when someone was drawing a bath. The noise of downtown was worst of all, especially when it was raining, because somehow the drumming rain enhanced the noise, even cars that were crawling along seemed to roar by and that sound lived on inside him, like a never-ending, thunderous circle. The only thing that was worse than sudden noises was sudden silence, because then the familiar realization returned, that if sound disappears then so does the world, and the quieter it got, the greater the feeling that he had lost contact with reality. He had long dreamed of finding the perfect silence, one with distant sounds. Lying in the bedroom and hearing a radio coming from the kitchen. Sitting in an empty restaurant with roadworks outside, watching the men work, the sound muffled by the large glass panes. He'd spent a lot of time thinking about that in the past, but now he had stopped doing that as well. He had slowly stopped caring about his own discomfort. He recalls the first time that feeling trickled through him. He was in the kitchen and suddenly smelled fire, and began to search the apartment. He went through the living room, following the odor of burnt electricity, caught sight of the electrical panel in the hall and noticed white smoke creeping through the cracks. He opened the box and found that it was burning inside. A very small fire, a cautious flame in the surface behind the fuses. He ran to the kitchen and filled a bucket with water, dashed back, and just as he was about to toss the water onto the fire he recalled something he'd learned in school, that water conducts electricity. And he recalled stories of people who dropped hair dryers in the bathtub and were fried. Maybe it would be a disaster to use water? He tried to blow out the fire, but that only made it burn stronger, he stood with the water in hand, helpless—until he exhaled, three seconds of complete calm, and poured out the water, full of certainty: it doesn't matter.

Nothing happened: the fire went out, the safeties flipped one by one, like popcorn. The next day, an electrician came to fix the box, all the dangerous electricity disappeared, but from that day on the feeling remained inside him: it didn't matter.

It wasn't that he had made a decision. He hadn't even formulated the thought in his mind; that was never it. Maybe it was like every other difficult thought: he pushed it away, preferring to make his brain empty to filling it with things he didn't know how to handle. He had been here at the pier many times before, to look out at the bay for a while before turning homeward again. He doesn't know what made this time any different from the others. He went to the edge and stood there for a moment. Gazed down at the water, saw the seaweed resting like a membrane over the enormous anchor cables. Eight inches of visibility, then it was black. He took off his clothes and placed them in a pile, the eyes of passersby lingering on him and moving on. And then he jumped in. There was no plan, no fine detail. He just decided to swim straight out for as long as he could, until he was sapped of energy. And he left the pier with its small-scale boat traffic, swam out into the open water. There was no breeze and the water was smooth as a mirror, but waves came in from the sea, full-bodied, the sea moved up and down around him, and he went with it, he was small and insignificant in the pitching waters, as if the sea hadn't yet decided what to do with him. The water grew colder as he went, and his strokes grew shorter. But he was a strong swimmer. His parents had sent him off to swim camp one summer. Everyone had known each other; he knew no one. The other kids were older than him. They had to swim in a line, he was slower than everyone else, when someone came up behind him a whistle sounded from the edge of the pool. "Give way!" And, panting, he grabbed the yellow lane marker, let someone pass. Later, in the showers, the smell of chlorine and his fingers wrinkled and the small puddles of water on the floor, gleaming in the fluorescent light, and the older boys running around and whipping each other with their towels and shouting, their voices echoing off the tile walls. They slept in a gym. The others had sleeping bags and sleeping mats, but Mom and Dad had forgotten to pack his. The swimming instructor let him borrow a blanket, and they unfolded the high-jump mat for him. The other kids started calling him "the king" because he lay there so majestically, up above everyone else. He cried silently for his parents when he was supposed to be sleeping. Gazed up at the ceiling, tracing the balance beams and the rings and the wall bars with his eyes. The last day was for theory. The swimming instructor gathered the wet children, lined them up at the edge of the pool, blew his whistle the second the kids got rowdy. He talked about what to do if you fell into cold water. And he stood at a blackboard, roaring so loud it sounded like a dog barking: "Orient yourself! Where are you going? Orient yourself! Where are you going? Orient yourself! Where are you going?"

Benjamin knew where he was going. He was going to the open sea, and it didn't matter what happened after that. He left the small islets behind, the sounds of the city were gone now, all he could hear was his own breathing and his hands scooping into the surface of the water.

A roar passed over the world, and when it ended there came a few seconds of silence. And then it happened again, a heart-stopping rumble, a thunderclap and a siren all at once, and the sound drilled right through him, he could feel it in the water, as if it came from the sea. And he turned around and saw the gigantic passenger ferry passing him, just fifteen yards away. The horn sounded a third time, and Benjamin's entire body was paralyzed for a second, the sound passed through flesh and bone, and he was back at the substation, hearing the explosion again and again, he felt Molly spasm in his arm, and he kept a firm hold on her, and the room turned blue and he felt the pressure at his back, and he thought that now he knew, now he knew how it feels to be blown to pieces. And then everything went black. And when he woke up, he did so with fire in his back.

Orient yourself! Where are you going?

Where are my brothers?

And he crawled over to Molly.

When the ferry horn sounded a fourth time, Benjamin screamed aloud, he heard his own gasps, he kept swimming. He swam straight out, the sea suddenly harsher, a breeze on his cold head. Then he saw them, two tiny heads in the water in front of him. He knew them immediately, he would recognize his brothers from half a mile away. He swam up beside them, saw Pierre concentrating, his head not far above the surface, looking at the little buoy farther off, bobbing in the water. "There's the buoy!" he called to Nils. "We're almost halfway!"

Pierre's eyes darted up to Benjamin's. "I'm scared," he said.

"Me too," Benjamin replied.

Nils was a ways ahead, Benjamin could see his head tilted back to keep water out of his mouth.

"Nils," said Benjamin. He didn't react, just kept swimming with his eyes on the sky. Benjamin caught up to his older brother, they breathed hard in each other's faces. They stopped in the water, the three boys. The sea was quiet, waiting.

"Your lips are blue," Benjamin said to Pierre.

"Yours too," said Pierre.

They grinned. He looked at Nils, his gentle smile. The boys

put their arms around each other, holding each other up in the water, and they pressed closer, warming each other's faces with their breath. They gazed into each other's eyes and he wasn't afraid anymore.

"I have to go now," said Benjamin. Nils nodded.

Pierre didn't want to let go. Benjamin placed a hand on his brother's cheek, he smiled at him, and then he pulled loose from his brothers and turned around again, facing the open sea, the cold on his legs biting and moving up to his thighs, his fatigue, he wasn't out of breath, just exhausted, he felt pinpricks in his shoulders and arms, and the water got closer and the waves, which had been big but friendly before, changed character, the sea leaned into him so powerfully that he gasped, and with that inhalation the sea poured inside of him, filled his stomach and airways and lungs, and in the seconds before he lost consciousness he stopped being anxious too, because he knew that at last, he could let go of the reality he'd been clinging to for so many years. He tumbled below the surface, limp and free, and when his heart stopped it was neither light nor dark, there was no glow at the end of any tunnel.

There was a gravel road.

22

2:00 A.M.

He tells his brothers that he's just going to use the bathroom, that he'll see them tomorrow. Pierre and Nils are bent double for a moment in Mom's hall, tying their shoelaces, and then they pile their mementos of Mom in their arms and stagger out into the dark stairwell. Benjamin watches them move toward the elevator, then closes the door. He really does use the bathroom, not because he needs to, but to mitigate his lie. He sees Mom's toiletries in the wide-open bathroom cabinet. Hand cream. A stuck piece of soap that has become one with the porcelain. A toothbrush, well used, almost brutalized. Traces of vomit in the sink. On the edge of the bathtub is the bottle of Chanel perfume, the one she bought herself years ago and worshipped so much that she never used it. Three lightbulbs over the sink, only one works. He stares at his reflection. He never looks in the mirror any more than is necessary, never makes eye contact with himself, always gazes past himself, at his chin or his nose, but now he lets his gaze linger. He sees his prominent mouth, his wide forehead. He remembers the time his dad jokingly said, "It's easy to imagine what you'd look like as a skull." When he was little, he was fascinated with his appearance. Stood at mirrors, entranced somehow. Once when he was home alone as a kid, he stood in front of the hall mirror and stared at himself for so long that eventually he was convinced he was looking at someone else. He wasn't frightened, he went back and tried again a number of times, but the moment never returned. Once, at the cottage, he sat on the kitchen floor with his legs outstretched on the rug, and he gazed at his lower body and suddenly felt like it wasn't his own. Those were someone else's legs, everything below his waist was just dead flesh that didn't belong to him. It was so real that he couldn't move. He reached for a piece of wood from the basket next to the kitchen stove and smacked himself on the thighs and feet, to feel something, take back the body parts that belonged to him.

He looks at himself in the mirror.

Tries to imagine what he would look like as a skull.

He goes to the living room and looks around the apartment, which is a mess after the three brothers' search for mementos to take with them. Photo albums open on the floor, cabinet doors agape in the kitchen, pictures taken down from the wall. It looks like a bunch of burglars have been here. He goes to the bedroom and sees the unmade bed, sheets still twisted from Mom's final bout with insomnia. He undresses, pauses for a moment, and then lies down in the bed. He doesn't want to go home. He wants to sleep here, in his mother's bed. An ashtray on the nightstand, cigarette butts at the bottom, and through them a line of stubbed, half-smoked cigarettes. The ashtray looks like a mohawk, a memory of Mom's last weeks, when she didn't even have the strength to smoke anymore.

He unfolds Mom's letter. In the faint glow of the bedside lamp, he reads it again. He hears his mother's voice, the one he knew so well, the one in which he could sense the tiniest detail, catch nuances even she wasn't aware of. He reads and pauses as he knows Mom would have done. He absorbs the text carefully, slowly, as if he won't ever see the letter again and has to memorize it. Then he places the letter on his chest. He turns out the light. He's four years old, in a bedroom he doesn't remember, on a bed he doesn't recognize. Mom pulls up his pajama top and tickles his belly, she says she's an ant and her middle and index fingers wander across his stomach, and Benjamin chokes with laughter, and Mom says here comes another ant, and now both hands are trailing across his stomach, and Benjamin twists and turns and kicks his legs wildly, accidentally hitting Mom in the head. She takes a few steps back, her hand to her forehead, muttering something to herself. Benjamin sits up on the edge of the bed. He says, Sorry, sorry, Mom, I didn't mean to. She says it's no big deal, still holding her hand to her head. She comes toward him, sees that he's crying, and hugs him, holding him: "It's okay, sweetheart. I'm fine."

Benjamin turns over in the bed. It's finally dark out, finally nighttime in the summer. He takes out his phone and calls Pierre. It rings for a long time before Pierre picks up. He can tell right away that Pierre's not himself, his voice is thick, congealed.

"Things are spinning," his brother says.

Pierre has just gotten into bed, he took some of the sleeping pills. He couldn't fall asleep and spotted the pack and thought he might as well.

"How many did you take?" Benjamin asks.

"One," he rushes to say, and then he adds, sounding uncertain and a little sly: "Maybe, maybe I did take two after all."

Pierre puts down the phone, the line crackles, Benjamin hears his slow footsteps across the floor, he picks something up and comes back.

"Two!" he cries. "I've got the pack here. I took two, and then I decided to have a competition with myself, to see how long I can stay awake."

He starts to giggle.

"It was going pretty well, but now . . ." He sighs, suddenly downtrodden. "Now I'm spinning."

Benjamin listens to a confused babbling through the phone, and then it stops, and all he can hear is Pierre breathing.

"Hello," says Benjamin. "Are you still there?"

"What the hell kind of lamp is this?" Pierre says. He's quiet for a few seconds. "How the hell do you turn it off?"

They end the call, and the phone screen emits its pale light into the room for a moment; then it goes out and the room is black. He tries to follow his therapist's advice for when he can't sleep. Take in a thought, observe it, and then get rid of it. Take in the next thought, observe it, and get rid of that one too. But it's that last step he can't manage, the first thought bumps into the second, and he drills down deeper into his associations, forgets the task at hand, and has to start over. He picks up his phone again, dials Nils's number. Nils answers as he always does, formally, by stating his last name.

"Did I wake you up?" Benjamin asks.

"No," Nils replies. "I'm in bed. Just about to turn out the lights." Benjamin can hear classical music playing faintly in the background.

"I read Mom's letter again," Benjamin says.

"Yeah," Nils says quietly. "It's so messed up . . ."

"What is?"

"That she couldn't say all of that while she was alive."

"I know."

Nils sounds so calm. So thoroughly grounded in what has just happened. Benjamin has always had the sense that Nils came through childhood okay because he never let it in. On occasion he has even wondered whether Nils may actually be happy. It seems like he is, now and then, on those rare occasions when they meet. But in unguarded moments, when his brother is refilling his coffee at the counter or standing by a window and gazing out, Benjamin can see sorrow glowing in Nils's eyes like a tiny phosphorescent flame.

"Can I ask you something?" Benjamin says.

"What?"

"The day you graduated high school, remember that?"

"Yeah."

"The morning after, you left for Central America. You were supposed to leave early in the morning. Do you remember?"

"Yeah."

"I was lying there in bed, listening to the sounds outside my door, I heard you leave. Why didn't you come in and say good-bye?"

"I wasn't allowed."

"Wasn't allowed?"

"Mom and Dad said you were sick. That we shouldn't bother you."

Neither of them speaks. The brothers' breathing, the quiet music in the background.

"See you tomorrow, Benjamin."

"It's already tomorrow."

"It's going to be okay."

"Yeah."

Late night becomes early morning.

He turns on the lamp again, sits up in Mom's bed, reads her letter again. A single page, covered front and back in her unmistakable handwriting, indistinct here and there but still crystal clear, without a doubt, a text that spins a web between decades, binding together everything from here to the cottage, a simple little letter full of everything they all had on the tips of their tongues but never spoke aloud.

The room shrinks.

He shuts his eyes and maybe he sleeps, he thinks so, because when he opens his eyes again the room is brighter. He looks at the window, he can see a scrap of sunlight on the very top of the building across the street. A tiny yellow corner of the gray concrete.

| **23** |

THE CURRENT

"I don't know how I got out of the water. I guess I was unconscious. My next memory is lying on the deck of a motorboat, I heard frantic voices around me, felt hands on my back. And I remember throwing up the water that had been in my lungs, all over my hands, and the water was warm and I thought it felt nice."

He had been staring at the floor as he told his story, but now he looked up at last, met her gaze. The therapist was jotting down notes in her journal, she hid them from him while they talked, but once in a while he saw the wild ink strokes she had made, little curlicues, half-finished sentences, an illegible keyword here and there.

"And I guess that's that," said Benjamin. "Then I ended up here, with you."

This was his third time seeing her. Two hours per session, according to a carefully delineated schedule. She had been very clear. In the past, people who had attempted suicide were almost exclusively given medication, she said. It was all about diagnoses and treatment. But now it was known that the patient's story was central—she had called Benjamin an expert, the one who knew the most about his own history, and hearing this had made him almost ridiculously elated, almost touched, maybe because she wasn't saying he was sick but, rather, the opposite: his own insights were crucial. She mostly just listened when he spoke, and sometimes she asked follow-up questions, some of them suggesting that she had spoken with his brothers, and he had nothing against that—he had given consent. Hour after hour of his account. That was all. The first time he came to the office, he had been surprised to find that there were two separate doors. One was for arriving and the other was for leaving. It was brilliant, like a system of gates that minimized the risk of encountering others. Still, Benjamin felt from the start that he learned more about the other patients than he would have liked. During his first visit he had to pee, and through the thin walls of the visitors' bathroom he could hear the conversations; just before he flushed he heard another person burst into tears. The office was large, one long corridor, and sorrows played out in a row behind its doors. Benjamin had knocked tentatively on the door the receptionist directed him to, and a voice came from within: "Yes?" The tone was one of surprise, as if she hadn't expected any visitors. And then he walked in. The therapist was a large woman in a small room with two deep easy chairs and a desk. And they sat across from each other, and he, the expert in himself, told his story and she listened, and the hours added up, painting a portrait of his childhood and adolescence, and now he was finished.

"Okay," she said, smiling at Benjamin.

"Okay," Benjamin said.

She bent over her journal, making yet another note. It had been fourteen days since Mom died. Twelve days since he decided to swim into the sea until he could swim no more. He spent the first twenty-four hours after his rescue in the hospital. The next day, they asked him if he planned to harm himself again, and when he said no he was telling the truth. They asked if he was prepared to undergo specialized psychiatry, and he said yes. He was allowed to return home. Then came days from which he remembers very little. He was at home and didn't go out. He remembers both of his brothers visiting him at the apartment. He remembers that Pierre brought a Swiss roll; he hadn't seen a Swiss roll since he was a child. He doesn't remember much about what they talked about, but he remembers that cake. It wasn't until a few days later, when he began therapy, that he slowly returned to himself. Three sessions spread out over a week. Their conversations anchored him in reality, grounded him.

"This is the third and final time we'll see each other," said the therapist. She glanced discreetly at the wall clock above his head. "I want us to devote the rest of our time to returning to a specific incident in your story—I hope that's okay with you."

"Of course," Benjamin replied.

"I'd like us to talk a little more about what happened at the substation."

There was a buzz from Benjamin's pants pocket; he took out his phone. A message from the group text Nils had created the afternoon Mom died. He had named the group "Mom" and Pierre had quickly renamed it "Mommy," Benjamin didn't quite understand why. As a joke? They never would have called her that when she was alive. He quickly read the text and put the phone down on the table next to his chair.

"You look a little confused," said the therapist.

"No, it's nothing," said Benjamin. He drank some of the water that was on the table. "Nils says he wants 'Piano Man' to be played at the funeral."

"'Piano Man'?" she asked.

"Yes, that song."

It was less than twenty-four hours until the funeral. Nils, as if obsessed, was making plans up to the last minute. He'd written in his text that it was Mom's favorite song, so it would be fitting, and Benjamin did have a memory of her playing it for the kids when they were little; she had shushed them all and asked them to listen carefully to the lyrics, and when it was over she said "Mwah!" and made a gesture with her hands to her lips, as if she were plucking a kiss from her mouth and tossing it into the room. Benjamin didn't care one way or the other if it was played at the funeral. But worry suddenly crept into him, because he knew what that text was the beginning of, he knew Pierre wouldn't let Nils off the hook now. Another buzz. Benjamin bent over to look.

"Haha," Pierre wrote.

And preparations for battle were underway, the three dots hopping in the texting app, eager points of Pierre's malice and Nils's umbrage dancing on the screen.

"What do you mean?" Nils wrote.

"Sorry. I thought you were joking. A song about a drunken artist playing the piano at a sleazy hotel bar? At Mom's funeral? Are you serious?"

"Mom loved it. How can that be wrong?"

"My favorite song is 'Thunderstruck' by AC/DC. Do you think I want it at my funeral?"

And then silence. Another minor injury to add to all the rest, another few delicate strands breaking between the brothers. He stuck his phone in his pocket.

"The funeral is tomorrow, already?" the therapist asked.

"Yes," he replied.

The therapist gave a gentle smile. "Anyway," she said, leaning forward in her chair. "I'd like to spend some more time at the substation."

"Okay," said Benjamin.

He didn't understand the reasoning behind this. He had told her everything he recalled about that day. He had told her everything he recalled from his childhood, sharing things that he'd experienced with his brothers but had never talked about with anyone, not even them. He had told her about birch whisks and buttercups, and he'd even shared his most difficult memories, things that changed him. The root cellar. Midsummer. His father's death. The idea was that this would help him understand himself, that he would see himself as the sum of his narrative. But now those stories were spread out before him and the therapist like Lego bricks, and Benjamin had no idea how to put them together. He knew that what he had done to himself two days after Mom's death was a result of all the rest of it. He just couldn't figure out how.

"And I think we have to take a big step now," said the therapist. "A step that might be difficult. Are you with me?"

"Okay."

"I want you to picture yourself at the substation."

He remembers the sight of the little building in the clearing. A path led up to it, faintly trampled, maybe not even trampled at all, maybe there was no path. The sound of mosquitoes and a bird very close by, and farther off, a hissing sound from the building, the quiet murmur of the electricity as it skimmed through the cables inside, tumbling around and dividing itself over to the cottages in the forest. From a distance, the building looked almost idyllic. Just a little cabin in the woods, and outside it a garden of power, poles in neat lines with their black hats gleaming in the afternoon sun. There was hardly any breeze. He remembers walking over roots that looked like ancient fingers.

"You're walking with your brothers and you approach the substation and you open the broken gate," says the therapist. "You're on the other side of the fence now. You go into the little building. Can you picture that?"

"Yes."

He remembers the black moisture on the walls. The roar of electricity flowing through the lines. A flickering light on the ceiling, giving a faint glow, he remembers thinking that was odd, that there was so much electricity and yet the light on the ceiling couldn't be any brighter? His brothers overexposed in the sunlight outside, they paled, he heard their voices, distant cries captured by the breeze, Nils told him to come back out. He said it was dangerous. As Benjamin approached the wall of electricity, their voices grew sharper, but nothing could reach him, their cries were only woolly calls in the distance, like echoes from across the lake on calm evenings when he and Pierre skipped rocks at the shore.

"You're standing inside the building," says the therapist. "You've got the dog in your arms and you're standing very close to the cables. What are you thinking?"

"That I'm invincible."

He remembers standing in the center of a raging current of power—and it didn't touch him! The feeling that he could do whatever he wanted, because nothing could get him. He was in the eye of a hurricane, everything around him was destroyed, but not a hair on his head was harmed. It was as if the current surging on the walls belonged to him now, he had broken into the core, he was victorious, all the power in here was now his own.

"You turn toward the door," says the therapist. "You look at your brothers. You're too close to the lines. You don't touch anything, and yet the current hits you."

He remembers the explosion. He remembers the seconds preceding it. He could guide the noise by moving his arms. He raised his hand to the current and the current answered him. Each time he reached toward the cables, his brothers' shouts were louder. He liked seeing them scared. He teased them, watched them as they stood with their fingers through the fencing. Then the room turned blue, the heat on his back, and the white explosion, he faded and disappeared.

"You wake up on the floor of the building," says the therapist. "You don't know how long you were unconscious. But eventually you wake up. Can you picture that?"

"Yes."

He remembers his cheek against the gritty floor. His back was missing—what else was gone? He didn't dare to look, because he didn't want to know what other parts of him were lost. He looked out the door, at the fence. Where are my brothers? They saw the explosion, they were witnesses to his being torn apart, they saw his body burning. And yet they left him. He remembers waking up and passing out again. He looked out, the sun had moved in the opposite direction, it became earlier in the afternoon.

"You've regained consciousness. You wake up. And now you discover the dog. She's not far away, on the floor. You crawl over to her, sit on the floor, and pick her up and hold her. Do you remember that?"

"Yes."

He remembers the shame.

The pain was nothing, he couldn't feel it anymore, his back was gone but he had lost the ability to feel anything but shame. He held her as the sun went up and down at superspeed outside, starry skies in various shapes signaling down at the little building. Clanging from the forest, loud and scraping, like the racket when a large structure sags and splinters, gentle, wild winds coming and going, fir trees swaying and stilling, animals stopping outside the building, peering in and moving on, and here he had always felt halfway outside reality, as if he were observing himself from some other place. Now he was not only in the center of himself, but in the center of the universe. He held her close, pressed her to his chest, she was cold.

"You're holding the dog," says the therapist. "You're holding her and looking down at her. Do you see her?"

"Yes," Benjamin replied.

"What do you see?"

He remembers hushing her gently, gingerly, as if she were asleep. He remembers crying over her face and how it looked like they were her tears. "It's not a dog you see, is it?" says the therapist. "When you picture her before you now, isn't it a little girl?"

Worlds rolled by outside the little building, he looked out at the gap where millennia passed by, and down at her, the little one, the one who had been bound to him from the start, who was under his protection, not only that day but every other day, and he sat there on the floor, held her lifeless body, weighed it in his arms, and he cried because he had failed at the only thing he had been put on earth to do.

"Isn't it your little sister in your arms?"

| **24** |

12:00 MIDNIGHT

A police car slowly plowed its way through the blue foliage, down the narrow tractor path that led to the property. Benjamin remembers it clearly, because he was on his knees on the lawn and none of what had happened had sunk in and that police car, those flashing lights, were like reality demanding to be let in, something from the outside world that wanted to know what he had done.

He remembers the two policewomen who got out. He remembers that Mom refused to let go of Molly when they wanted to examine her. They talked to Dad, he remembers the sound of their murmurs in the dim twilight, and Dad pointed discreetly at Benjamin, and then they all came over to him, approaching from different directions. He remembers that both women were kind, they laid a blanket over him in the summer-evening chill, asked questions, and were patient with him when he couldn't answer. He remembers that another police car arrived a while later. And after that came an ambulance. And then came a procession of other vehicles, a truck from the electric company, other cars, they parked crookedly along the sloping tractor path. People vanished up into the forest, toward the substation, and came back. Strangers stood in the kitchen, using the phone.

Suddenly there were so many people. This place, which had always been deserted, where no one but the family ever set foot, was now crawling with people and everyone wanted to get inside him, wanted to make his crime real with their questions.

He's been taking walks again.

From the therapy office along the old tollgates in the south end, across the bridges, through the deserted alleys of Gamla Stan and along the quays, all the way downtown. He walked until the summer night fell, and now he's passing the subway entrance with the broken escalator once again, the sidewalk cafés where he used to sit and drink with Mom. When he arrives at Mom's front door, his brothers are there waiting for him.

"Have you been crying?" Nils asks.

"No, no," Benjamin replies.

They walk into the stairwell, sensing each other's bodies in the silence of the elevator. Mom's nameplate has already been removed. It's a callous detail that's generally in keeping with all other contact Nils has had with the landlord. Two days after Nils reported Mom's death and stated that they wanted to end the lease, he got a text from the landlord saying that they had inspected the apartment and found that it didn't merely "smell of smoke," as Nils had maintained when he'd described the condition—it was to be considered "smoke damaged" and must be sanitized immediately. The apartment had to be emptied sooner than planned, and that's why the brothers are here now, in the middle of the night, the day before Mom's funeral, to rescue some last mementos of Mom before the apartment is cleaned out tomorrow and it all disappears.

Nils unlocks the door and goes around turning on lights; the apartment begins to glow. Mom only bought lamps from the fifties and set them up on every conceivable surface; all these light sources in brown, yellow, and orange bathe the apartment in light reminiscent of the evening sun on a dock in June. The brothers slowly drift through the apartment to find things to remember Mom by, but Benjamin remains standing in the hall. He looks at his brothers, watches them search tentatively through bookcases and empty chests of drawers, and he finds that they remind him of their younger selves on Easter: little pajama boys on the hunt for chocolate eggs Dad hid in the furniture. Nils finds a small wooden sculpture and takes it down off the shelf. Pierre spots Mom's photo albums and sits on the living room floor; immediately sucked in, he has soon forgotten why they're here.

"Look at this," he says to Nils, holding out one of the photos. Nils laughs and sits down next to his brother. They sit there on the floor, in their stocking feet, like children in overgrown bodies, as if they have become adults despite themselves, and they look in wonder at photographs of themselves as children, trying to understand what happened. Benjamin goes to the kitchen. Something crunches underfoot, specks of marmalade gleaming softly in the light of the ceiling fixture. Little greetings from Mom everywhere, tooth marks on the pointy, knife-sharpened pencils on the kitchen table. The white-bottomed saucepans that have had milk burned onto them throughout the decades. Lipstick on the edge of the coffee cup in the sink. A single plate with an outline of tomato sauce. He opens the fridge, and yet another source of yellow light spreads its glow across the kitchen floor, the door racks full of medicine, small bottles with information leaflets stuck on like wings, white plastic blister packs, foil tabs and red triangles flashing signals into the room. Mom's presence is total, and as he digs through the items he feels guilty for doing this without asking permission first. He opens the freezer. Every shelf is wedged full of single-serving packages of pierogi. It was an emergency measure undertaken by the brothers a month or so ago, to get Mom to eat more. They took Mom to the store, walked through the freezer section to spark her enthusiasm, showed her different meals. All she wanted was pierogi.

"You can't eat nothing but pierogi," said Nils.

"Sure I can," said Mom.

They came home with three bags full of pierogi, and as they loaded it all into the freezer Mom stood alongside, saying "Delicious" and "Fantastic" with every new box they stuffed in. And he remembers the messages she sent each evening, when she reported her intake—"A two-pierogi day!"—in little attacks of wanting to reassure them. But just as often, she wanted to get them worked up. She used her health as a way to control them. "I weigh eighty-eight pounds!"

Like a baby pig.

"There's quite a bit of food here," Benjamin calls into the apartment, and Nils and Pierre get up and come to the kitchen.

"Wow," Nils says. "Should we split it in thirds?"

"What do you mean?" Pierre says.

"Should we divide up the pierogi?" Nils asks.

"You mean you want to take Mom's food home and eat it?" Pierre says. "Are you serious?"

Nils takes a box and shows it to Pierre.

"There's forty pounds of food in the freezer," he says. "All of it new and fresh. Do you want us to just toss it because it reminds us of Mom, or something?"

"No, fine, but you can have all of it," says Pierre.

"I'm saying I don't want it all. We can divide it up."

"I'm good."

Pierre walks off, Nils watching him as he enters the bathroom. Nils and Pierre have made small piles on the living room floor. Some porcelain, a bowl, and a small framed picture. In Pierre's pile Nils can see Mom's piggy bank, which is a jam jar she cleaned out and set on the hall table and filled with spare change. The jar is full of coins and the occasional bill. The idea was for the brothers to gather here and take items of sentimental value. Pierre is taking cash.

"Can I have this?" Pierre says from the bathroom. He holds up a blister pack of Mom's sleeping pills.

"Go for it," says Nils.

He drops the packet onto his pile. Benjamin looks at the jar of money again. A feeling from his childhood, something unfair between the brothers. He wants to point out to Pierre that it isn't an artifact he wants to take home, it's money. It's their inheritance. But he can't predict Pierre's reaction, it's been a long time since he knew his brother inside and out. He looks at his brothers as they walk around the apartment. All the years they've spent a minimal amount of time together, and now this intensive contact, with a constant strain at the base of it. He doesn't know what his brothers are really like, beyond the practical level. He can't picture them outside the context of Mom's death. He remembers one time when he arranged to meet up with them, on the anniversary of Dad's death. They had stood by his grave for a moment, in silence, and then they sat down at a café for coffee and a pastry. Benjamin asked if his brothers were doing all right, and they gave curt and unengaged replies, quick affirmatives between bites, and Benjamin told them for the first time that he wasn't doing all right. They expressed sympathy, of course, but it was clear they didn't want to talk about it. Benjamin said he thought he was sad as an adult because of things that had happened to all of them in their childhood. At that, Pierre laughed and said, "I whistle my way to the shower each morning." Maybe it was true, maybe Pierre does do that. Maybe he's the only one of the brothers who hasn't recovered. Maybe that's why being around them makes him feel so awful these days? And somehow, they've exchanged roles. When they were kids, it was always him and Pierre—Nils off to the side, or three yards behind. He remembers one time when they were little, sitting in the car, all three of them, and Nils found a piece of gum one of the brothers had grown tired of and stuck to the back of the front seat. He took a pen and started digging at it, he pried it off the seat and popped it into his mouth. Benjamin and Pierre looked on in disgust, and then they looked at each other, made discreet faces, as they'd done so many times before, and Nils said calmly, "Don't you think I can see what you're doing?" Maybe he was imagining it, but for the past week he's felt like his brothers have made him a victim of the same thing, that they've been exchanging glances that weren't meant for him.

"Oh my God!"

It's Nils, shouting from the bedroom.

Pierre and Benjamin go to him. He's standing at Mom's little desk, which faces the window. He's pulled out the top drawer. In his hand is an envelope, and he holds it out to them, Mom's unmistakable handwriting on it. It says: *If I die.*

They sit next to each other on Mom's bed, three brothers in a row, and read her letter.

To my sons.

As I write this letter, Molly is turning twenty. I've been to the memorial, I brought a flower. It's always more apparent around her birthday, or when the anniversary of her death is approaching. I am living a parallel life with her. When she turned seven, I bought a cake and ate it in the park and I could picture her in front of me, making circles around me, happy and wobbly on a bike, the wind in her hair. When she became a teenager, I sometimes imagined that I could see her through the gap of the bathroom door. I was watching her in secret as she put on her makeup, bending toward the mirror, full of concentration. She was going out on the town with friends.

I continue to be a parent in silence. I have read that it's normal, so I allow myself this. It's not sad; maybe it's the opposite. I can re-create her in such detail that it becomes true. I can be the mother of my daughter again, for a little while.

They told me grief is a process, with phases. And that life awaits me on the other side. Not the same life, of course, but a different life. It wasn't true. Grief isn't a process, it's a state of being. It never changes, it sits there like a rock.

And grief makes you mute.

Pierre and Nils. So many times I have meant to talk to you, that in the end I thought I actually had. I must have. What kind of mother wouldn't? I'm sorry for everything I never said.

Benjamin. You had to carry the heaviest burden. I'm saddest for you. I've never blamed you, not once. I just haven't been able to tell you that. If, in my muteness throughout the years, I could only manage to say one thing to you, it would have been: It wasn't your fault.

I watch you sometimes when we meet. You're standing off to the side a little, often in a corner, observing. You've always been the observer and you still try to take responsibility for the rest of us. Sometimes I imagine things about you too, about who you would have become if this hadn't happened. I often think about that afternoon when you came out of the forest with Molly in your arms. I have such clear memories of her, her cold cheek, her curls in the sun. But I can't see you anywhere before me. I don't know where you went, I don't know who took care of you.

I don't have a will, because I have nothing to pass on. I don't care about the details surrounding my death. But I do have one last wish. Take me back to the cottage. Spread my ashes down by the lake.

But I don't want you to do it for my sake—I know I have forfeited every right to ask you all for anything. I want you to do it for your sake. Get in the car, take the long way. That's how I want to picture you, together. All those hours in the car, in the solitude down by the lake, in the sauna in the evenings, when it's just you and no one else is listening in. I want you to do what we never did: talk to each other.

I'm not letting you read this until I'm dead, because I'm afraid you'll think what I did to you can't be forgiven. I don't know, but can we just pretend I'm able to be with her now. That I can hold her again. And that you'll come later, and then I'll have a fresh chance to love you.

Mom

Nils places the letter in his lap. Pierre stands up suddenly, walks to the balcony, searching his pockets for his cigarettes as he goes. His two brothers follow slowly. There they stand, side by side, the ones who remain, gazing out at the sleeping city. Pierre is smoking hard, the cigarette a glowing point in the darkness. Benjamin reaches for the cigarette and Pierre hands it to him. He takes a drag, passes it on to Nils. Pierre laughs. Nils's gentle smile in the dim light. They let the cigarette wander and look at one another there on the balcony, and they don't need to talk right now, a brief nod, or maybe just the thought of a nod. They already know, already have the journey inside them, as if it has already happened, the journey that must take them to the point of impact, step by step, backward through their story, in order to survive one last time.

Acknowledgments

Ever since I first began to write, my dream has been to one day have a book published in the United States. I have many people to thank for the fact that this far-fetched dream is now a reality.

First and foremost, thank you to Daniel Sandström, my publisher at Albert Bonniers Förlag in Sweden. It is no small thing to meet a person with whom you feel such immediate kinship. There has been something almost mysterious about it. As though we have known each other much longer, as though we have bantered about reading and literature since we were young. I also want to thank my editor Sara Arvidsson, who has been a benign force throughout our work with this book. I have always been finicky when it comes to text; I like the thought that a piece of writing is never really finished, ever, that there is always something more that can be done. But I have met my match in Sara, who is even more fastidious than I am.

I have also had the great fortune to be surrounded by friends who have offered to read my work in progress. I want to name one friend in particular: Fredrik Backman. I don't know how many hours of his time I have hijacked during the writing of this novel. One hundred? Two hundred? That his next book is a tad bit delayed may be my fault. I also want to thank Sigge Eklund, Calle Schulman, Klas Lindberg, Josefine Sundström, Magnus Alselind, and Fredrik Wikingsson.

I also want to thank my agent, Astri von Arbin Ahlander, at Ahlander Agency. All writers in Sweden want to work with Astri, but she hardly wants to work with anyone. Therefore, I am grateful that she believed in me and my writing. Astri also forever changed my view of what an agent does. I thought an agent hawked titles at book fairs and then that was the end of it. Well, Astri has indeed done that—that the book is now sold to so many countries is exclusively her and her team's doing—but she is also one of the most perceptive readers I know and her thoughts on the novel throughout the writing process have been absolutely invaluable.

I also want to thank Lee Boudreaux at Doubleday, who has taken the brothers to her heart and who has given them a home in the U.S. She possesses a kind of enthusiasm I have never before met in this otherwise rather reserved publishing industry. Personally, I have always enjoyed writing in all caps and adding a tail of exclamation points—but Lee out-enthuses me!!!

And, finally, I want to thank my most important person, my wife, Amanda. She is my first reader and my last reader. I don't deliver a single line into the world without her first having read it. I can't manage without her, not in my life and not in my writing.

Alex Schulman is a bestselling author and journalist and the co-host of Sweden's most popular podcast. *The Survivors,* which has sold in more than thirty countries, is his fifth novel and marks his international debut. He lives in Sweden with his wife and their three children.